Enid Blyton™

Naughty Amelia Jane!

Amelia Jane Gets Into Trouble!

2 Books in 1!

EGMONT

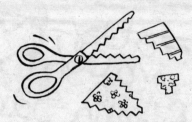

EGMONT

We bring stories to life

Naughty Amelia Jane First published in Great Britain 1946 by Newnes
Amelia Jane Gets Into Trouble First published in Great Britain
1954 by Newnes as part of *More About Amelia Jane!*
This edition published 2007
by Egmont UK Limited
239 Kensington High Street
London W8 6SA

Naughty Amelia Jane Text copyright © 1946 Enid Blyton Ltd, a Chorion company
Amelia Jane Gets Into Trouble Text copyright © 1954 Enid Blyton Ltd,
a Chorion company
Illustration copyright © 2001 Enid Blyton Limited
Illustrations by Deborah Allwright

The Enid Blyton signature is a registered trademark
of Enid Blyton Ltd, a Chorion company.

ISBN 978 1 4052 2951 7

www.egmont.co.uk

5 7 9 10 8 6 4

A CIP catalogue record for this title is available from the British Library

Printed and bound in Great Britain by the CPI Group

More Enid Blyton published by Egmont Books

Naughty Amelia Jane!

EGMONT

Contents

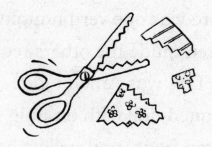

Naughty Amelia Jane

The toys in the nursery were very friendly with the small pixies who lived in the bushes below the nursery window. The pixies had no wings, but they managed to climb up the tall pear tree and get in at the window whenever it was open. So you can guess that the toys and the pixies had many a good game!

There was one very naughty toy, who often made the others really angry. This was Amelia Jane, a big, long-legged doll with an ugly face, a bright red frock, and yellow hair. She hadn't come from a shop, like the others, but had been made at home. Shop-toys nearly always have good manners, and know how to behave themselves – but Amelia Jane, not being a shop-toy, had no manners at all, and didn't care what she said or did!

Once she poured a jug of milk down Tom the toy soldier's neck, and that made him wet and uncomfortable for two days. Another time she threw a woollen ball up so

high that it went into the goldfish
globe, and made the poor goldfish
jump almost out of his skin. Then,
when the teddy bear climbed up to get
the ball out of the water, Amelia Jane

climbed up behind him, gave him a push – and there was the poor bear, spluttering away in the water, and trying his hardest to swim, whilst the goldfish darted at him in fury.

Dear dear, how Amelia Jane laughed, and how all the other toys shouted at her! Whatever would she do next?

The next thing she did was to catch a bee in a matchbox, and then, when the sailor doll needed matches, she gave him the matchbox, pretending that there were matches inside. You can imagine how scared

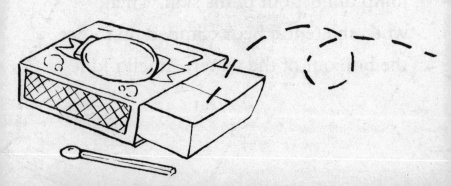

he was when a bee flew out and stung him on the nose!

'Amelia Jane, you are a perfect nuisance,' said the toys angrily. 'Can't you settle down and be good like us? One day you will do something that will get us all into trouble!'

'Pooh!' said Amelia Jane rudely. 'I shan't!'

But she did do something very

naughty indeed the next time.

She was hunting about in Nanny's work-basket for a thimble to play with, when she came across Nanny's scissors. Ho! Now she could have a fine game of cutting!

So she took the scissors and began to snip-snip-snip everything! The other toys were sitting in a corner playing a game of snap, and they didn't notice at first what Amelia Jane was doing. They wouldn't let Amelia play snap with them because she said 'Snap!' when it wasn't, and took away all their cards.

So Amelia Jane had a lovely time all by herself. She snipped a hole in the curtains, and then she snipped

another! Then she went to the hearth-
rug and cut a whole corner off that!
Then she found Nanny's handkerchief
on the floor, and do you know, she cut
it into twenty-two tiny pieces! It was
one of Nanny's best hankies too, with
a pretty lace edge. But Amelia Jane
didn't care about that!

Then she went to the carpet and

began to snip little bits of it here and there. The carpet was a green one with red roses, and wherever Amelia could see a rose, she snipped! Wasn't it dreadful of her?

The toys took no notice. They were having such a lovely game. Amelia grew cross with them for being happy without her. So what do you suppose she did? She went up behind the pink rabbit and snipped his tail off!

Goodness! You should have seen how he jumped!

'Oooooooh!' he yelled. 'She's snipped my tail off! Look! Oh, the wicked, wicked doll!'

'And look what else she's done!'

cried the toys in horror, pointing to the spoilt hanky, the snipped rug, and the cut carpet. 'And look, she's spoilt the curtains too. Oh, what trouble we shall get into! Nanny will know it must be the toys, and she will throw us all into the dustbin! Oh!'

The toys stared in horror at all that the naughty doll had done. The pink rabbit cried bitterly, for he felt dreadful without a tail. Oh dear! How he would be laughed at, now that he hadn't a tail! Tom the toy soldier put his arm round him and comforted him.

'Don't worry, Bunny,' he said. 'We shall all love you just the same, even if you don't wear a tail, and look rather like a guinea-pig!'

The pink rabbit cried all the more loudly when he heard that. 'I don't want to be like a guinea-pig!' he wept. 'I want to be like a rabbit! I hate Amelia Jane! Punish her, Tom! She is a very wicked doll!'

Amelia Jane laughed. She loved doing naughty things. She liked seeing all the toys staring in horror at the mischief she had done. Ha, Ha! That would teach them to play snap without her!

'Give me those scissors,' said Tom sternly.

'Shan't!' said Amelia Jane, twirling them round in her big hand.

'I said, "Give me those scissors!" '

ordered the toy soldier.

'I said "Shan't!" ' said Amelia
Jane, 'and if you talk to me like that,
Tom, I'll chop your hat into little
pieces! Then you'll look horrid!'

'You naughty, wicked doll!' said
Tom, in a fury. But he didn't dare to
try to take the scissors away, for they
had very sharp points, and he really
was afraid that Amelia Jane would cut
up his lovely hat. He was very proud
of it, and he didn't want anything to
happen to it.

'Whatever shall we do?' said the
teddy bear. The toys all looked at one
another in despair.

Then they heard a little scraping
noise at the window, and they saw

their friends, the pixies, creeping in at the crack at the bottom.

'Hallo, Toys! You look very miserable!' said the pixies, scrambling down from the window-seat to the floor. 'What's the matter? Have you lost a pound and found a penny?'

'No,' said the toys. 'Just look here, pixies, at what Amelia Jane has done!'

'I say!' said the pixies, staring at all the damage. 'Why did you let her have scissors? And look, she still has them. You ought to take them away from her before she does any more mischief.'

'She won't let us have them,' said Tom. 'She says she will chop my hat into little pieces if I try to take them from her.'

'Oho, we'll soon see to that!' said the biggest pixie at once. 'Scissors, come to me!'

He waved his little gold wand – and immediately the scissors flew out of Amelia Jane's hand and went to the pixie. He caught them and gave them to Tom.

'Oh, thank you,' said the toys gratefully. 'I suppose you couldn't help us to mend all these dreadful holes and slits that Amelia has made?'

'Oh yes, I think so,' said the biggest pixie. 'We'll just go and get our needles and thread, and come back to help you. We'll sew everything so that you won't see even a tiny stitch! We are very clever at stitching, you know. Once we sewed all the petals on a daisy that had lost hers in a rainstorm – and you really couldn't see that they were not growing! As for that handkerchief, we'll use a bit of magic for that, and all the bits will join together so that Nanny will never know it has been cut!'

The pixies fetched their needles and thread, and soon they were sitting on the carpet and on the rug, mending all the slits and cuts, and two of them mended the curtains. Then the biggest pixie put a spell into his needle and sewed on the bunny's tail again. It didn't hurt a bit because of the spell. The bunny was so grateful.

The handkerchief was mended too –
and everything was put right.

'There!' said the pixies, in delight.
'We've done all we can!'

'We can't thank you enough!' said
the toys. 'You may be sure that if ever
we can help you in return we will!'

'As for Amelia Jane,' said the biggest
pixie, 'I should keep her a prisoner in
the toy-cupboard until she says she is
sorry and won't be naughty any more.
Here is a spell that will keep her there!'

Tom took the spell. It was in a little
box, and when it was taken out and
blown over Amelia, she had to stay
where she was put. The toys
surrounded the naughty doll, pushed

her into the cupboard, and then blew the spell at her. She couldn't move her legs! There she had to stay!

At first she was very angry. Then she was frightened, and begged to be set free. She saw the toys going happily about their play, and she wanted to join them. It was dreadfully dull in the toy-cupboard all alone except for a box of bricks that never said a word.

'I'm sorry, Toys! Do set me free!' begged Amelia Jane. 'I will try very hard not to be naughty any more.'

'If we could be sure you would do good things and not naughty ones, *we would* set you free,' said Tom. 'But we don't trust you. You have never done a good or brave thing all the time you have been with us.'

Amelia Jane was just going to answer him when there came a tapping at the window. The toys looked up. A small red robin was there. He looked most excited.

'What is it?' shouted the toys, swarming up to the window-seat.

'It's the pixies!' said the robin. 'They have been attacked by the goblins! They have hidden in the old hollow tree, but the goblins are cutting it down! Can you rescue them?'

'How?' said Tom, upset and bothered to hear such bad news.

'I don't know,' said the robin. 'You'll have to think of something – but hurry, because at any moment the goblins may get them!'

He flew off, and the toys crowded together, all talking at once.

'Toys, Toys, I have a plan!' cried Amelia Jane from the cupboard. 'Let me fly the toy aeroplane out of the window. It will frighten the goblins terribly, and they are sure to run away. Then, before they come back, the pixies can get into the aeroplane and I'll fly it safely back here!'

'All right!' shouted the toys, excited. 'It's a good idea. Set her free, Tom.'

So Amelia Jane was set free. The aeroplane was run up to her, and she got in. Rr-rr-rr-rr-rr! It shot up into

the air and out of the window. How
exciting it was! Amelia was a bit
afraid of falling out, but she managed
to guide the aeroplane to the hollow
tree. Then down she flew – and all the
little goblins who were cutting down
the tree to get at the pixies inside,
cried out in horror:

'Run! Run! The aeroplane is
coming down on top of us!'

They scattered in fright. Amelia stopped the aeroplane and landed by the hollow tree. She called to the pixies:

'Pixies! Quickly! Get into my aeroplane! I've come to rescue you!'

The pixies all shot out of the hollow tree at once and clambered into the plane. When the goblins saw what was happening they gave a shout of rage and ran to the aeroplane at once – but it was too late. Rr-rr-rr-rr-rr! It rose into the air, and flew straight back to the nursery window. In two minutes the pixies were safe in the nursery with the toys, and *how* pleased they were!

'Amelia Jane has turned over a

new leaf,' said the pixies, in surprise. 'Brave Amelia Jane! Thank you so much for rescuing us!'

'Don't mention it!' said Amelia. 'I am trying very hard to be good now.'

And you will be pleased to hear that she certainly *was* good for a little while, but I'm afraid it didn't last for very long!

Amelia Jane Gets a Shock

Well, for a little while Amelia Jane was very good – and then, oh dear, she forgot all her promises, and became really naughty! The things she did!

She took a needle and cotton out of Nanny's work-basket, and sewed up the sleeves of the teddy bear's new coat when he wasn't looking. So when he

went to put on his coat, he simply
could *not* put his arms through the
sleeves anyhow! He just couldn't find
the way in – because the sleeves were
sewn up! How Amelia Jane laughed to
see him!

The next night she hid behind the
curtain and began to mew like a cat.
The toys were not very fond of Tibs
the cat, because he sometimes chewed
them. So they all stopped playing and
looked round to see where Tibs was.

'I can hear him mewing!'
said the teddy bear. 'He
must be behind the
door.'

But he wasn't.
Amelia mewed

again. The toys hunted all about for the cat. They even looked in the coal-scuttle, and under the hearth-rug, which made Amelia laugh till she nearly choked! She mewed again, very loudly.

'Where is that cat!' cried Tom the toy soldier, in despair. 'We've looked everywhere! Is he behind the curtain?'

'No, there's only Amelia Jane there!' said the golden-haired doll, looking. 'There's no cat.'

Well, of course, they didn't find any cat at all! And Amelia Jane didn't tell them it was she who had been mewing, so to this day they wonder where Tibs hid himself that night!

Then Amelia Jane saw a soda-water siphon left in a corner of the room. She knew how it worked, because she had seen Nanny using one. Oh, what fun it would be to squirt all the toys! She stole towards it – picked it up, and dear me, it *was* heavy! She ran at the surprised Tom, pressed down the handle – and out gushed the soda-water all over him!

'Ow! Ooh!' he shouted, in astonishment. 'What is it? What is it? Amelia Jane, you ought to be ashamed of yourself!'

But she wasn't a bit ashamed. She was just enjoying herself thoroughly! She ran after the teddy bear and soaked him with soda-water too. She squirted lots over the clockwork mouse, and made him so wet that for two days his clockwork went wrong, and he couldn't be wound up. She squirted the pink rabbit, and he got into the wastepaper basket and couldn't get out, which worried him very much, because he was so afraid that Jane, the cleaner, would throw him away the next day! But she didn't, which was very lucky.

'Amelia Jane is up to her tricks again,' said the clockwork clown, frowning. 'We shall have no peace at all. What shall we do?'

'Take away her key!' said the clockwork mouse.

'She hasn't one, silly!' said Tom.

'Lock her in the cupboard!' said the teddy bear.

'She knows how to undo it from the inside,' said the pink rabbit gloomily.

Nobody spoke for a whole minute. They were all thinking hard.

Then the clockwork clown gave a little laugh. 'I know!' he said. 'I've thought of an idea. It's quite simple, but it might work.'

'What?' cried everyone.

'Let's polish Amelia Jane's shoes underneath and make them very, very slippery,' said the clown. 'Then, if she begins to run after us with soda-water siphons or things like that, down she'll go!'

'But she won't like that,' said the golden-haired doll, who was rather tender-hearted.

'Well, *we* don't like the tricks she plays on *us*!' said Tom. 'We'll do it, Clown! When she next takes her shoes off we'll polish them underneath till they are as slippery as glass!'

The very next night Amelia Jane took off her shoes because she said her feet were hot. She put the shoes into a corner and then danced round the nursery in her stockinged feet, enjoying herself. The clown picked up the shoes and ran away to the back of the toy-cupboard with them. He had a tiny duster there, and a little bit of polish he had taken out of Jane's polish jar when the nursery had been cleaned out. Aha, Amelia Jane, you'll be sorry for all your tricks!

The clown polished and rubbed, rubbed and polished. The soles of the shoes shone. They were as slippery as could be! The clown put them back and waited for Amelia Jane to put them on. This she very soon did, for she had stepped on a pin and pricked her foot! As she put her shoes on, she thought out a naughty trick!

I'll run after all the toys with that pin I trod on! she thought. Oooh! That will make them rush away into all the corners! What fun it will be to frighten them!

She buttoned her shoes and took the nasty long pin into her hand. Then she stood up and looked round, her naughty eyes gleaming. I'll run

after that fat little teddy bear! she thought. So off she went, straight at the teddy bear, holding the pin out in front of her.

'Amelia Jane, put that pin down!' shouted the teddy bear in fright – but before Amelia Jane had taken three steps, her very, very slippery shoes slid along the ground and down she fell, bumpity-bump! She *was* so surprised!

Up she got again and took a few more steps towards the teddy bear – but her shoes slipped and down she fell! Bumpity-bump! She hit her head on the fender!

'What's the matter with the carpet?' cried Amelia Jane in a rage. 'It keeps making me fall down!'

'Ha ha! ho ho!' laughed the toys. 'Perhaps there is slippery magic about, Amelia Jane!'

'Oh, I believe you toys have something to do with it!' shouted the angry doll. Up she got and took the pin in her hand again. 'I'll show you what happens to people who put slippery magic on the floor! Here comes my pin!'

She tried to run at Tom, who was laughing so much that the tears ran all down his face. But down she went again, bumpity-bump – and oh my, the pin stuck into her knee! Yes, it really did – she fell on it!

How Amelia Jane squealed! How Amelia Jane wept! 'Oh, the horrid pin! Oh, how it hurts!' she cried.

'Well, Amelia Jane, it serves you right,' said the pink rabbit. 'You were going to prick *us* with that pin and now it's pricked *you*! You know how it feels!'

Amelia Jane threw the pin away in a rage. The clown picked it up and flung it into the fire! He wasn't going to have pins about the nursery!

Amelia Jane got up again. 'I'm going to bandage my knee where the pin pricked it,' she said. She ran to the toy cupboard – but before she was halfway there, her slippery shoes slid away beneath her – and down she sat with a dreadful bumpity-bumpity-bump!

The toys laughed. Amelia Jane cried bitterly. The golden-haired doll felt sorry for her. 'Don't cry any more, Amelia Jane,' she said. 'Take your shoes off and you won't fall again. We played a trick on you – but you can't complain because you have so often tricked *us*! You should not play jokes on other people if you can't take a joke yourself!'

Amelia Jane took her shoes off. She saw how the clown had polished them underneath, and she went very red. She knew quite well she could not grumble if people were unkind – because she too had been unkind.

'I'll try and be good, Toys,' she said at last. 'It's difficult for me, because I'm not a shop-toy like you, so I haven't learnt good manners and nice ways. But I may be good one day!'

The toys thought it was nice of her to say all that. The golden-haired doll came to help her bandage her knee. The clown put a bandage round her head where she had bumped it. She looked so funny that they didn't know

whether to laugh or cry at her.

Amelia Jane did enjoy being fussed! She was as nice as could be to the toys – but oh dear, oh dear, I do somehow feel perfectly certain that she can't be good for long!

Amelia Jane
at the Sea

Once it happened that Amelia Jane, the big, naughty doll, was taken down to the seaside with some of the other toys. The clockwork clown went, the brown teddy bear, Tom the toy soldier, and the golden-haired doll. They went in the car with the children, and they were all most excited.

'I shall dig in the sand and throw it

over everybody!' said naughty Amelia Jane. 'And I shall get my pail and fill it full of water and pour it down Tom's neck! Ho, won't he jump!'

'You'll do nothing of the sort, Amelia Jane,' said Tom at once. 'You know how often you've promised to be good. Well, just you remember your promise.'

'And I shall push the clockwork clown into a rock-pool and make him sit down there with all his clothes on,' said Amelia Jane, with a naughty giggle.

'You mustn't!' cried the clown, in alarm. 'If you do that, my clockwork will get rusty and I shan't wind up properly – then I won't be able to walk any more, or turn head-over-heels!'

The children often took the toys down to the beach with them. After dinner the children went to have a rest, and the toys were left in a sheltered corner of the beach. No one ever came there, so the children knew they were quite safe. And it was whilst the toys were left alone there that Amelia Jane behaved so very badly. She did all she said she would, and more too.

She threw sand all over the golden-haired doll, and it went into her eyes dreadfully. She cried, and Tom had to find his handkerchief and comfort her. Whilst he was patting the doll on the back, and wiping the sand out of her eyes, Amelia Jane was filling her pail from a pool.

She crept up behind Tom and tipped the pail of cold sea-water all down his neck!

'Ooooo-ow-oooo!' yelled Tom, jumping about twelve centimetres into the air with fright. 'You wicked doll, Amelia Jane! I told you not to do that!'

Amelia Jane thought it was such a funny joke that she rolled over and over on the sand, laughing. The clockwork clown, who had seen all that had happened, remembered what she had said she would do to him, and he ran away to hide. He really was dreadfully afraid Amelia Jane would push him into a pool. Amelia looked for him. He had hidden himself under a clump of seaweed, so she couldn't see him – but she saw the brown teddy bear!

He was walking round the edge of a deep pool, looking at the crabs there. Amelia Jane crept up behind him. She gave him a push – SPLASH! The teddy landed in the pool and sat right down in the water.

'Oooooo-ow-ooooo!' he gasped, his mouth full of salty water. Amelia Jane laughed till the tears ran down her face.

'You are very naughty and unkind,' said the clockwork clown, poking his head out of the seaweed nearby. 'You are a most dreadful doll. Hi, Tom, come and help me push Amelia Jane into the water!'

'I shan't let you!' said Amelia Jane, at once. 'I shall paddle out to sea and sit on that rock over there. I am bigger than any of you, and I can get through the deep water easily. You won't be able to follow me. I shall be quite safe. Ha ha to you, clockwork clown!'

Amelia Jane had no shoes or socks on. She lifted up her red skirt and stepped into the waves. She waded out towards the big, big rock that showed itself some way out. It was covered with green seaweed. The teddy shook the water from his fur and ran after Amelia, splashing through the waves. But he was afraid of getting drowned, and he soon came back. Amelia was a very big doll, so she could easily get to the rock. The water did not come to more than her knees.

She reached the rock and climbed up. She waved to the others.

'I'm the king of the castle!' she shouted, dancing on the rock. 'You can't get me! I shall stay here and have a nice nap!'

She lay down on the soft green seaweed. The hot sun had dried it well. It was like a soft bed.

Amelia fell asleep. When the children came out to play, they didn't miss her. They had new spades and they wanted to dig a big castle.

They took no notice of any of the other toys, and didn't even see how wet the teddy bear was. They dug and dug and dug.

They had tea on the beach and then they dug again. When it was time to go home they collected their toys and set off up the beach. They had the clockwork clown, the bear, the toy soldier and the golden-haired doll – but they didn't have Amelia Jane. They had forgotten all about her.

And what about Amelia Jane? She was still asleep on the rock! The tide was now coming in – and it crept higher and higher over the rock. Soon it would reach Amelia's toes. Soon a big wave would break right over the rock on top of Amelia – and then what would happen to her?

Amelia woke up. She sat up on the rock and looked round. When she saw how the tide was coming in, she was in a dreadful fright. The water was too deep to paddle through now. She couldn't swim. Oh dear!

Amelia Jane stood and yelled for help. 'Save me, somebody!' she cried. 'Save me!' But there was no one to save her. Poor Amelia Jane!

The other toys were sitting on a shelf, watching the children go to bed. Nobody thought of Amelia Jane. They were only too glad to forget her.

But when the children were safely in bed, Tom the toy soldier suddenly looked round – and saw no Amelia. For a moment he wondered where she was – and then he remembered! She had been left on the rock – and the tide was coming in. Oooooo!

'I say, Toys,' said Tom, 'Amelia Jane's on the rock – and the sea will soon cover it right over!'

Now you might think that the clown, the golden-haired doll, and Tom would say, 'And serve Amelia right!' – but they didn't. They all looked at one another in alarm. Amelia was naughty – and she had played tricks on them – but they could not let anything horrid happen to her.

'What can we do?' asked the clown. He got down from the shelf and ran to the window. From there he could quite well see the rock on which Amelia stood, shouting for help.

'We must save her!' said the golden-haired doll.

'But how?' asked Tom.

'I know!' said the clown suddenly.

'We will take the children's toy ship – and sail it to the rock. We shall just get there in time. Hurry!'

The toy soldier and the clown caught hold of the toy ship, which lay on the floor. They ran out of the door with the golden-haired doll, and tore down to the beach. They put the boat into the water.

Tom got in. The golden-haired doll got in. The clockwork clown pushed off, and then jumped in himself. Tom arranged the white sails so that the wind filled them. The clown took the rudder and guided the little ship.

The tide was coming in fast. It was a long, long way now to the rock.

Amelia Jane was very frightened. A big wave had washed right over the rock and had wetted her to the waist. Amelia was afraid that the next one would wash her right off the rock into the big sea.

'Help! Help!' she shouted, as another big wave came over the rock. Amelia held on to some seaweed. The sea wetted her right up to her shoulders. Oooh! It was so cold! She knew now how cold Tom must have felt when she poured water down his neck that morning!

'We're coming, Amelia Jane; we're coming!' shouted the toys. Amelia Jane heard them.

She looked over the waves and saw

 the three toys in the
sailing-ship. It bobbed
up and down as it came,
for the sea was quite
rough.

'Oh, you good
creatures!' sobbed Amelia Jane. 'I
don't deserve to be rescued – I was so
unkind to you – but oh, I'm *so* glad to
see you!'

The ship sailed quite near to the
rock. The clown was careful not to let
it strike the rock – for that would
mean a wreck. 'Jump, Amelia, jump
into the ship!' he called. 'We can't
come any nearer!'

Amelia Jane jumped. It was a good
jump. She landed right in the middle

of the boat. It swayed about, and then
as the clown turned it into the wind,
the sails filled and the little ship sailed
towards the shore again.

'You'll soon be safe home,' said the
golden-haired doll kindly. 'Don't cry,
Amelia Jane.'

'I won't tease you any
more, any of you,'
wept Amelia. 'It
was so kind of
you to

remember I was on the rock and come
to rescue me. Thank you ever and
ever so much.'

The ship reached the sand. Tom
jumped out and pulled it in. The
golden-haired doll jumped out and
helped poor, wet, cold Amelia Jane
out. The clown jumped out last of all
– and then they carried the ship back
to the nursery again.

Tom took Amelia Jane down to the
kitchen fire and dried her. Then back
to the nursery they went, and soon fell
asleep after their exciting day.

And was Amelia Jane kinder to the
toys after that? Yes, very much kinder,
all the time they were away at the
sea. But alas! When they went back

home again, Amelia Jane forgot all her good ways. Read on and you will see!

Amelia Jane and the Cowboy Doll

Now one day a funny little doll came to stay with the toys in the nursery. He was a cowboy doll. He didn't belong to the children who owned the nursery, he was just lent to them for a few days.

He was dressed in shaggy trousers, leather tunic, and a cowboy hat. He was very smart indeed, and the other toys were a bit afraid of him.

He could ride the old wooden horse, and made it gallop as fast as could be round and round the nursery! Once he even climbed up on to the big rocking-horse and made it rock so fast that the horse hrrumphed in surprise, and Nanny came running

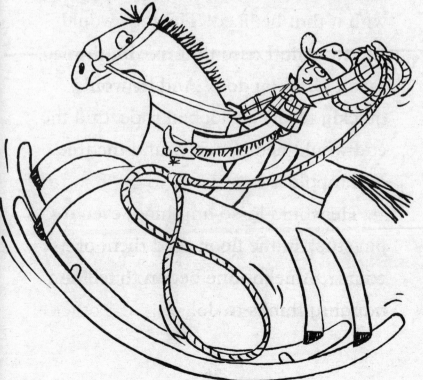

in to see what all the noise was about!

The cowboy doll only just had time to hop off the horse and lie down on the floor, where he had been put by the children!

Another thing he could do was rather marvellous. He had a long rope, and he could lasso anything with it that he liked! The toys would say to him, 'Lasso that tree on the toy farm, Cowboy doll!' And he would quickly throw his looped rope, and the end would neatly curl round the tree and topple it over!

He would lasso anything, even a pin stuck in the floor. And then, of course, Amelia Jane began to tell him naughty things to do!

'Cowboy doll, do lasso the clockwork mouse!' she whispered. 'Oh do! Look, he is over there, sniffing at that brick!'

The cowboy doll grinned. He had a most wicked face. He threw his rope neatly, and the loop at the end dropped right over the mouse's head – click!

The mouse gave a squeak of surprise and tried to run away, but the rope held him tight! He was very frightened.

'You shouldn't tell the cowboy doll to do that, Amelia Jane,' said Tom crossly. 'Why *must* you always get into mischief? Go and untie the mouse, quickly.'

'You go, Tom,' said Amelia Jane, giggling as she thought of more mischief. 'You are better at knots than I am!'

Well, the mouse was squealing so loudly that Tom really thought he had better go and help. So off he went, and Amelia Jane nudged the cowboy doll and whispered to him:

'Where's your other rope? Lasso Tom! He will get such a shock!'

So when Tom was bending over the mouse, trying to undo the loop of rope round him, there came a whizzing noise through the air, and another rope fell neatly right round Tom's waist – click! It pinned his arms to his sides and he couldn't move!

What a shock he got!

'You're my prisoner, Tom!' grinned the cowboy doll. 'Come over here!'

'I won't!' scowled Tom. 'Let me go!'

But he had to walk over to the cowboy doll and Amelia Jane because the cowboy pulled hard at the rope, and Tom had to come with it! He was so angry!

Amelia Jane thought lassoing was a lovely thing to do. She wanted to learn, and the cowboy doll said he would teach her.

'No, you are not to teach her,' said the golden-haired doll sharply. 'She is quite naughty enough without learning any more tricks. You are

NOT to teach her!'

But the cowboy doll was not used
to obeying other people, so he took no
notice at all. He began to teach
Amelia Jane, and she tried very hard
to learn.

Soon she could throw a rope
wonderfully well, and then, what a
time the poor toys had! They never
knew when a rope was going to come
whizzing through
the air after them,
falling over their
heads and
shoulders! It was
most worrying.

Amelia Jane
practised hard, but

she could not get quite so good at it
as the cowboy doll.

Once she sent the rope flying
through the air to catch the teddy
bear as he walked along, and she
missed him and got the rope round
the chimney of the dolls' house.

Of course, she pulled too hard, and
the chimney came off and fell on top
of the bear's head. He was very cross
indeed, and threw the chimney at

Amelia Jane.
She threw it
back, and it
almost hit the
nursery cat on
the nose. He was
most surprised,

and looked as if he would eat Amelia Jane. So she ran into the cupboard till the cat had gone down to the kitchen for his dinner.

The toys made her climb up to the dolls' house roof and put the chimney on again. She didn't like that at all, but she had to do it. But even then she wouldn't stop lassoing things.

She lassoed the humming-top when it was spinning and made it fall down in a fright. She threw her rope at a cow in the farmyard, but caught the farmer himself and jerked him so high in the air that he really thought he was flying. He came down in the coal-scuttle and was very angry about it. He told all his cows to go and bite Amelia Jane, and she had to climb up on to a shelf out of their way.

Another time she was very naughty indeed. She thought she would lasso Mister Noah, who lived in the wooden ark, and give him a shock. He didn't like Amelia Jane, and wouldn't even say good morning to her when he met her. So Amelia waited for him to come out with all his animals.

'I'll lasso him now!' she whispered to the cowboy doll, with a grin. 'Watch me!'

She sent the rope through the air – whizz! But she missed Mister Noah, and the rope fell neatly round two

tigers and two bears! How they
roared and growled! They bit through
the rope in a twinkling, left the line of
animals, and tore over to where
Amelia was standing with the cowboy
doll.

The bears bit the cowboy doll's
shaggy trousers so hard that they

made a hole in them. The tigers
scratched Amelia Jane on her legs,
and you should have heard her yell!

'It serves you right,' said Tom, who had been watching. 'We've told you ever so many times not to keep lassoing people.'

So for a little while Amelia Jane was good, but then something happened that made her bad again.

Somebody left a bag of sweets on the nursery mantelpiece. They belonged to one of the children, and Nanny had put them there. Amelia Jane saw them and looked longingly at them, for she loved eating lots of sweets and chocolates.

How could she possibly get those sweets? She looked up at the mantelpiece and thought hard. The clock ticked away there. The goldfish globe winked back. It stood on the mantelpiece too, and was full of little black tadpoles that the children had found in the ponds. The china cat stood there too, watching the tadpoles wriggling about. And just by the cat was that bag of sweets.

'Oh, I know how I can get them!' said Amelia suddenly. 'I can lasso them with the cowboy's rope! Cowboy doll, where are you? Will you lend me your rope for a moment?'

The cowboy doll untied it. He always kept it tied round his waist. He gave it to Amelia Jane and asked her what she wanted it for.

'I'm going to lasso that bag of sweets on the mantelpiece and get it down here!' said naughty Amelia. 'Then we'll share the sweets, Cowboy doll!'

'You'd better let *me* do the lassoing,' said the cowboy. 'You'll only go and lasso the cat or the clock, Amelia Jane!'

'No, *I* want to do it,' said Amelia. She looked up at the mantelpiece and swung the rope carefully. Whizz! It flew up to the mantelpiece! It missed the bag of sweets. It missed the clock. It just missed the china cat, but it caught the goldfish bowl! It fell neatly round it. The rope was tight – it pulled at the bowl – it toppled it over!

The watching toys gave a shriek! The water poured out of the bowl – all over Amelia and the cowboy doll, who were just underneath! Tadpoles fell down their necks and flopped on to the floor! The bowl fell off too, and all the toys thought it would smash on the floor.

But no! It was too clever for that! It fell on to Amelia Jane's head, and there she stood, wet through, with the glass bowl on her head like an extra big hat!

Well, really, the toys simply couldn't *help* laughing! She looked too funny, and the cowboy doll, too, was soaked from head to foot. He was

trying to get a tadpole which had
fallen down his back and was tickling
him dreadfully.

'Don't stand there laughing like
this,' said Tom suddenly. 'Those
tadpoles will die out of water. Quick,
get something to put them into.'

The toys looked round for
something but all they could think of
was Amelia Jane's teacup. She was a
big doll, so she had a very big cup.
The toys put some water in it and
then picked up the poor wriggling
tadpoles. They found the one down
the cowboy's neck, and took two from
Amelia's neck as well. Dear, dear,
what an excitement there was!

'What do you want to bother with

silly tadpoles for, when Amelia Jane and I are all wet through!' cried the cowboy doll crossly. 'Please dry us.'

'It is more important to save the tadpoles than to bother about *you*,' said the clown. 'You can dry yourselves. It was your own fault that all this happened. Amelia Jane had no right to try and lasso sweets that didn't belong to her!'

Amelia squeezed out of her wet things and took the bowl off her head. It was rather a tight fit, and at first she thought she might have to wear the bowl all her life! That did give her a shock. She stood by the fire and tried to dry herself. She felt very cold and sad. The cowboy doll was wet too, and very angry.

'You *are* silly,' he said to Amelia Jane. 'Why didn't you let me do the lassoing? I could have got the bag of sweets then, but all we got was cold water and tadpoles!'

Amelia Jane said nothing, but dear me, when she found that her teacup was full of swimming tadpoles she was horrified.

'How can I ever drink out of my nice cup again?' she wept. 'It will be all tadpoley.'

'Amelia Jane, stop being silly,' said Tom sternly. 'You have made enough mischief without being stupid too. What do you suppose Nanny will say when she finds the tadpoles upset and the bowl on the rug?'

Nanny said a lot. She simply could *not* understand what had happened! At first she thought it was the cat who had done it. But no, Tibs had been in the kitchen all the time. And then she caught sight of the cowboy doll who was standing in a corner, still very wet.

'I believe it's you, with your lasso, you naughty doll!' she said. 'Back you go to your own home!'

'Perhaps Amelia Jane will be good now that the cowboy doll has gone,' said the teddy to the clown. But I don't expect she will – do you?

Amelia Jane and the Plasticine

Now Amelia Jane had been good for a long time – so good that the golden-haired doll really wondered if Amelia was ill. But she wasn't ill; as the clown said, 'She was just boiling up for some more mischief!'

Amelia Jane had found the box of plasticine in the cupboard, and every night she played with the plasticine.

She sat in a corner by herself, and the other toys took no notice of her at all. Amelia Jane was clever with the plasticine – she could make flowers and shells and tables and chairs and all kinds of things, just as you can.

And then, of course, naughty ideas began to come into her mind. She had heard the teddy bear complaining that he had no tail. Suppose she made him one and stuck it on when he was asleep? He would think he had grown a tail, and what fun it would be to see him walking about proudly, showing off his beautiful new tail! What would he say when it came off?

Amelia Jane made a beautiful long tail of plasticine. It was brown to match the teddy bear's fur, and it had some pretty little blue spots here and there. Amelia Jane made some marks on it to make it look furry. It was finished at last. Amelia Jane grinned to herself and waited till she saw the teddy bear asleep in a corner.

Then she crept up to him with the plasticine tail. Nobody was about.

Amelia Jane quickly pressed one end of the tail on to the teddy bear's back. It stuck nicely. Then the naughty doll ran back to her place in the cupboard.

Presently the clockwork clown walked along to talk to the bear. He saw the tail, and he stared as if he couldn't believe his eyes!

'Hie, Teddy, Teddy, wake up!' he shouted in excitement. 'You've grown a fine tail! You have really!'

The teddy woke up with a jump. When he saw his new tail, curling round him like a cat's, he was so surprised that he couldn't say a word at first. Then he got up and bent himself over to have a look at it.

'A tail at last!' he said. 'A real tail!

I always thought I might grow one, and now I have!'

'Tom, come and look at Teddy's beautiful new tail!' cried the clown. 'Do come! It's a fine one!'

Tom came, and the golden-haired doll – and Amelia went too.

'It's magnificent,' said Tom.

'It makes you look really handsome, Teddy,' said the golden-haired doll.

'How clever of you to grow it all by yourself!' said naughty Amelia Jane.

'Wasn't it clever of me!' said Teddy proudly, and he walked about showing his new tail to everyone. The clockwork mouse loved it, and the yellow duck said it was the longest she had ever seen. The bear was so happy that his boot-button eyes shone like lamps.

Not long afterwards the toys all sat down together to have cups of cocoa which the clockwork mouse had made for them on the stove in the dolls' house. Amelia Jane sat down beside the teddy – and whatever do you suppose she did? When the others were not looking she took hold of the bear's plasticine tail and with her clever fingers she made the end of it into a snake's head! Fancy that! It looked exactly like a snake now, with its mouth open and two little holes for eyes!

Tom saw it first and gave a shriek!
'Oooh! Look! Your tail has turned into
a snake, Teddy!'

The bear looked down in alarm –
and when he saw the snake's head on
the end of his tail he jumped up with a
yell.

'Oh! Go away, snake, go away!'

he shouted, and he ran to the other side of the room. But, of course, his tail followed him, for  it was stuck on to him – and it looked as if the snake was running after him backwards! Poor Teddy! He was so frightened. He didn't like snakes at all, and to have his new tail turning into one seemed very dreadful to him.

Well, Amelia Jane laughed till she cried. It seemed funny to her to see the teddy bear rushing about with a snake-tail! The toys thought her very unkind to laugh, and the golden-haired doll shouted at her. But as

Amelia Jane could shout twice as hard, that wasn't much good!

'Take your tail off, silly, if you're afraid of it!' called Amelia Jane.

'How can you take off a thing that's growing on you, stupid!' yelled back the teddy.

Amelia Jane ran to the bear and jerked at his tail. It came off quite easily, of course, for it was only plasticine. She threw it out of the window. The toys looked on in surprise. Then they all cheered Amelia.

'How brave of you, Amelia Jane! How good of you to do that! Did it hurt, Teddy?'

'Not a bit,' said Teddy, in surprise.

'Oh, thank you, Amelia Jane. The snake might have bitten you. You are very brave.'

Amelia Jane didn't tell the toys that the tail had only been plasticine made by herself. No – the naughty doll said nothing at all, but let the toys make a fuss of her.

I'll think of another plasticine trick, she thought gleefully. And, as you can guess, it wasn't very long before she did!

She made a set of nice little chairs, all with seats and backs and four neat little legs. Then she went to the paintbox and got the red paint. She painted those little chairs a bright red, and really, they looked simply lovely when she had finished. But, of course, you couldn't sit down on them because they were only made of plasticine and would crumple up at once!

But they didn't look as if they were made of plasticine when they were bright red. They looked like wooden chairs. Amelia Jane set them all out neatly in the middle of the floor.

'What are those chairs for?' asked Tom, in surprise.

'I'm going to have a party,' said Amelia Jane, and she got a table from the dolls' house. Then she called to the toys, 'Do come and join my party. The cakes haven't come yet but they'll be here soon. Just come and sit down and wait a while, Toys!'

The toys were pleased, for they loved any sort of a party. They came running over to Amelia Jane. Even the clockwork mouse came, and so did the old blue rabbit who had only one eye and no whiskers at all.

'Do sit down,' said Amelia, waving her hand to the red chairs. 'I hope there are enough seats for you all!'

Everyone sat down – but oh, what a shock they got! Tom's chair sank down at once, all its legs broken! He landed with such a bump on the ground! The golden-haired

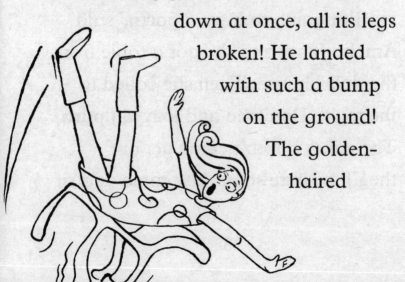

doll's chair tipped over backwards, and she bumped her head, and sat so hard on the plasticine that it stuck to her pretty blue frock. The clockwork mouse's chair crumpled up and he fell off and lost his key.

One by one all the red chairs gave way and tipped out the surprised toys. The clown didn't know what was happening and he clutched the back of his chair so hard that he squeezed up the plasticine it was made of and got it all over his arms! What a shock for him!

Amelia Jane thought it was so funny! She laughed and laughed and laughed.

'It isn't funny,' said Tom angrily.

'Is this a trick instead of a party?'

'Yes,' said Amelia Jane. 'Oh, Tom you did look funny tumbling on to the floor!'

'I suppose there are no cakes coming after all,' said the clown fiercely. 'And I suppose too that it was you who stuck on the teddy bear's tail, and made it of plasticine! You are a wicked doll and you deserve to be frightened yourself!'

'Oh, you can't frighten me!' said Amelia Jane. 'I'm not afraid of anything!'

But she was, you know – she was afraid of beetles! The toys knew this, and they made up their minds to punish her! They went to the

plasticine box, and the clown, who was clever with his fingers, made lots of big beetles, all with feelers on their heads and six legs under their bodies! The clown painted them black.

'This isn't a very kind thing to do,' said the clown, as he finished the last beetle, 'but really, Amelia Jane is so naughty that we must teach her a lesson. Where is she?'

'In the toy-cupboard, reading,' said the mouse. The clown took up the beetles and put them here and there on the floor. Then he called Amelia Jane.

'Amelia, Amelia, come quickly!'

Amelia Jane put down her book and rushed out of the cupboard – but when she saw those plasticine beetles she gave such a yell!

'Oooh! Ow! Beetles! Where have they come from? Take them away!'

The bear had tied a bit of black cotton to one beetle and he suddenly jerked this. The beetle jumped, and Amelia Jane screamed: 'It's coming after me! It's coming after me! Oooooooh!'

She rushed back into the toy cupboard and crouched in the darkest corner. And do you know, she didn't come out of the cupboard for two days, so the toys had a lovely time playing together without wondering what mischief Amelia Jane was up to!

They have taken away the beetles, of course, but Amelia Jane doesn't know that! She'll think twice before she gets into mischief again, won't she!

Stop it, Amelia Jane!

You might think that Amelia Jane would grow out of her bad ways, but she didn't. The day soon came when she felt bad again. It was the day that the pop-gun came to the nursery. The children had bought it and had been playing with it. It was great fun.

It was a wooden gun that had a cork fitted in at the end of it. When you pressed the trigger the cork flew out with a pop, but it didn't go far, because it was tied on to the gun with a piece of string. The children set up their wooden soldiers in a row and shot them down – bang! – with the pop-gun. The soldiers didn't mind, because it was what they were made for.

But when Amelia Jane got hold of the pop-gun that night and began shooting the cork at everyone, there was trouble!

'Stop it, Amelia Jane!' shouted the clockwork clown angrily, when his cap flew off into the coal-scuttle, shot there by the cork.

'Stop it, Amelia Jane!' cried Tom when he got the cork in his eye.

'Stop it, Amelia Jane!' squealed the engine. 'You're making my funnel loose with that cork – it keeps hitting it!'

But do you suppose Amelia Jane stopped? Of course not! She was enjoying herself far too much!

She shot at the castle of bricks and down they all fell! She shot at everything in the toy farmyard, and trees, animals, and farmer fell over flat. She shot at the clockwork mouse and gave him such a fright that he ran into the dolls' house and hid under a bed. Nobody could get him out.

The clockwork clown called the other toys to him. 'We've got to stop Amelia Jane!' he said. 'I'm tired of all this popping. That cork doesn't do much damage but it stings all the same.'

'What about shooting Amelia Jane?' asked Tom eagerly. 'I'd like to do that.'

'Oh, she won't let that pop-gun go, you may be sure of that!' said the teddy bear.

'Well, there's a funny old gun in the cupboard that the children got out of a cracker,' said the clockwork clown. 'Why not shoot at her with that?'

'Because it doesn't shoot, silly,'

said the bear. 'I've tried it heaps of times.'

'If it only made a pop it would do,' said the clown gloomily. 'We don't really want to shoot Amelia Jane – only to frighten her and make her stop popping the cork-gun at us.'

'Well, that old gun doesn't shoot and it doesn't make a pop either,' said Tom.

Then the bear had an idea. 'Listen!' he whispered, so that Amelia Jane wouldn't hear. 'I know where there is a packet of balloons! Couldn't we get them – and blow them up – and let Tom hide behind the curtain with them? Then I could hold the gun and point it at Amelia Jane – and at

the same moment Tom could prick a
balloon and burst it! Then it would go
– *bang*! just like a gun – and frighten
Amelia Jane!'

Everyone thought that was a
splendid idea. So Tom got the packet
of balloons and organised the toys to
blow them up. They hid behind the
curtains with the balloons. There were

five. The bear
found the gun and
polished it up.
Amelia Jane saw
him and laughed.

'*That* old gun
won't shoot!' she
said, and she
aimed the pop-gun at Teddy and shot
the cork so hard that one of his ears
went crooked. He was very angry.

'Oh, so you think this old gun
won't shoot!' he said. 'Well, you're
wrong!'

He pointed the gun at Amelia Jane
– and at the same moment Tom dug a
pin into one of the blown-up balloons
behind the curtain.

Bang! went the balloon – and Amelia Jane gave a shriek. She really thought the gun that Teddy was holding had gone off!

'I'm shot! I'm shot!' yelled Amelia Jane in a fright. Everyone laughed. Teddy pointed the gun at the naughty doll again. Bang! went another balloon behind the curtains. Amelia Jane squealed and ran away.

'I'm shot again! I'm shot again!' she yelled. Teddy laughed so

much that he nearly dropped the gun.

'Do you promise not to shoot anybody with that pop-gun again?' he said.

'No, I don't!' said Amelia Jane.

'All right then!' said Teddy, and he pointed the gun at her again. 'I'll go on shooting at *you* then.'

Bang! went a third balloon behind the curtain, and Amelia Jane screamed, 'I'm shot! I'm shot! He's shot me three times!'

Bang! went another balloon, and Bang! went the fifth balloon. Amelia Jane screamed so loudly that she quite deafened everyone. She fled into the toy-cupboard and wept bitterly.

'I won't shoot anyone any more.

Here's the old pop-gun!' she cried and she threw it out of the cupboard to the teddy bear. 'Stop shooting me! I'm wounded everywhere!'

When Amelia Jane next came out of the toy-cupboard the toys stared in astonishment – for the big doll had bandaged her arms and legs and head. She did look funny!

'You shot me five times and wounded me,' said Amelia Jane in a hurt voice. 'You ought to be very sorry.'

But the toys laughed and laughed and laughed. How could she be wounded when it was only balloons that went off pop and not the gun? Oh, Amelia Jane, you are just a humbug!

Amelia Jane Up the Chimney

Into the nursery where naughty
Amelia Jane lived, came a little black
kitten one day. Its eyes were green, its
tail was fat and long, and its little
paddy-paws were like velvet.

All the toys loved the kitten at once
– but Amelia Jane loved it most of all!
How she cuddled it! How she fussed
it! How she stroked it from ears to

tail-tip and tickled it under its soft black chin!

The kitten belonged to the housekeeper. It was a pretty, gentle little thing, and it let the toys do what they liked with it. The teddy found it a buttery crumb to nibble. The clockwork clown turned head over heels seven times running to make it laugh. Tom found the dolls' hairbrush and brushed its fur till it shone.

But Amelia Jane wanted the kitten all to herself. She pushed away the other toys, and as she was bigger

than they were they fell down, flop!
That was the worst of Amelia – she
was always so rough!

'*I* want this kitten!' said Amelia
Jane. 'Tiddles, Tiddles, purr to me,
and to no one else!'

'You are very selfish, Amelia Jane,'
said Tom. Amelia Jane stuck out her
elbow and pushed him again. Down
he went, flip-flop! You couldn't do
anything with Amelia Jane when she
was feeling like that.

'This kitten is mine when it comes
into our nursery,' said Amelia.
'Nobody else is to play with it then.'

Well, the kitten quite enjoyed being
made a fuss of by Amelia, but it did
want to play with the other toys

sometimes. Amelia just wouldn't let it. She caught it and put it on her knee to stroke as soon as ever it ran over to Tom or Teddy.

And one day Amelia Jane thought she would like to dress the kitten up in clothes out of the dolls' chest-of-drawers! Quite a lot of clean dolls' clothes were kept there. It was really rather exciting to pull open the drawers and see the dear little coats and dresses, the fussy little bonnets with ribbons on, the socks and the shoes of all colours!

Amelia Jane pulled out the whole lot. She would, of course!

'Just look at that!' groaned Tom. 'Untidy creature! She'll never put those clothes back again neatly. *We* shall have to do that!'

Amelia Jane soon had all the clothes on the floor. She wondered which would fit the little black kitten. What fun to dress her up, she thought!

'This dress will fit you nicely, Tiddles,' she said, picking up a little red frock. 'Oh, you will look sweet in it. And this yellow coat will fit you, too – and this little bonnet with ribbons! Oh, what a darling kitten you will look!'

'Mee-ow,' said Tiddles, not at all liking the idea of being dressed up by Amelia Jane. 'Mee-ow! I'm off!'

She shot to the nursery door – but Amelia Jane was too quick. She reached out her hand and caught poor Tiddles. 'You come here!' she said. 'I'm going to make you look really sweet!'

Well, Tiddles had to sit and be dressed up. First Amelia put on the little red frock and did all the buttons up the back. Then she put on the yellow coat. She tied a ribbon round Tiddles' waist. Then she put the bonnet on Tiddles' little black head and tied it on firmly.

'There!' she said. 'You are now a little dolly cat! You look lovely! Look, everybody!'

Everybody came to look. They couldn't help thinking that Tiddles really did look rather sweet – but

Tiddles hated it! She struggled and wriggled and tried her hardest to scrape off her bonnet. She didn't like anything over her ears. She couldn't hear properly.

'Now, you shall look at yourself in the mirror, Tiddles,' said Amelia Jane, and she carried the dressed-up kitten to the big mirror.

The kitten looked at herself – and when she saw herself looking so very strange, with a bonnet on her ears, and a coat and dress hiding her black fur, she was afraid.

'Mee-ow! It isn't me!' she said in a fright, and she rushed away to go downstairs to the housekeeper. But Amelia Jane pushed the door shut.

'You're not to go away, Tiddles,' she said. 'We want to see you walking about nicely in your new clothes.'

But that was just what Tiddles couldn't and wouldn't do! She caught sight of herself in the mirror again and ran off in terror. She was so frightened that she meant to get out of the nursery somehow! But how could she? The door was shut. The window was shut.

'Oh, where can I go-ee-ow?' mewed poor Tiddles.

Now it was summer-time, so there was no fire in the nursery grate. Tiddles leapt over the guard, and in a moment she scrabbled up the chimney and was gone!

The toys stared at one another in alarm. What would happen to Tiddles up the chimney?

'Are you all right, Tiddles?' called Tom, sticking his head up the chimney.

'No-ee-oh-ee-ow!' wailed poor Tiddles, who was more frightened than ever up the dark chimney. She didn't dare to go up and she didn't dare to go down! Poor Tiddles!

The toys turned fiercely on naughty Amelia Jane. 'It's your fault!' shouted Teddy. 'You would dress her up and frighten her, just to amuse yourself. Now what are we to do?'

'Oh-ee-ow-ee-oh!' wailed Tiddles, up the chimney.

'I know! We'll make Amelia Jane go up the chimney and fetch Tiddles!' cried Tom. 'That's what we'll do!'

'I won't go,' said Amelia Jane.

'Oh yes, you will!' said Teddy. 'Come on, everyone. Push Amelia up the chimney!'

But they couldn't get the big doll to go. She just wouldn't be pushed. Just as the toys were going to have another push at Amelia, someone opened the nursery door. It was the housekeeper!

The toys at once lay down flat on the floor and kept quite still.

'I wonder where that kitten of mine is,' said the housekeeper, looking round the nursery. 'I thought I heard her mewing up here.'

'Oh-ee-ow-ee-ow!' wailed Tiddles from the chimney. The housekeeper looked astonished. 'I believe she's up the chimney!' she said. Then someone called her from downstairs and she hurried away.

Now Amelia Jane, although she really was a very naughty doll, was feeling most uncomfortable about poor Tiddles, for she was fond of her.

As soon as the
housekeeper had
gone she ran
across to the
fireplace, climbed
over the guard, and
looked up the
chimney.

'I'm going up the
chimney to rescue
Tiddles,' she said to the
surprised toys. 'I'm not
going because you tried
to push me up – I'm going because I
don't like Tiddles to be frightened.'

And up the chimney went Amelia
Jane! The toys listened to her
scrabbling her way up the long, dark,

sooty chimney. Bits of soot fell down and one bit hit the teddy on the nose. 'The chimney wants sweeping,' he said.

'Looks as if Amelia is sweeping it!' said Tom, as another bit of soot rolled down.

At last Amelia Jane reached Tiddles who sat in a sooty corner, trembling. Amelia Jane put her arm round the kitten and hugged her. 'I'll help you to get down,' she said.

But dear me, that wasn't easy! Amelia Jane lost her way in the chimney, which joined all sorts of other chimneys here and there! Tiddles clung to her with all her claws and Amelia felt as if she was being pricked with twenty needles!

Now, very soon, the housekeeper came into the nursery again, and who do you suppose was with her? The sweep! Yes – the housekeeper had told him a kitten was up the chimney, and he had said he would try to sweep her out very gently.

He screwed on the handles of his big brush one after another, and the brush went higher and higher up the chimney. Amelia Jane heard it coming. She didn't know the chimney was being swept. The toys had all rushed into the cupboard when they heard the housekeeper and the sweep coming upstairs! They hadn't had time to tell her anything.

'Oooh! What's this coming up the chimney?' suddenly said Amelia, as she dimly saw something black and hairy coming nearer and nearer. She didn't know it was the sweep's round black brush! 'Oooh! It's got whiskers! It's touched me! It's pushing me!'

Poor Amelia Jane! She was just as frightened as the kitten had been when it first ran up the chimney! She couldn't get away from the brush. It lifted her and the kitten up, up, and up!

'It's caught me, it's caught me!' wept Amelia. 'I didn't know a whiskery thing lived in chimneys!'

The brush swept Amelia Jane and the kitten right out of the chimney

into the air! The kitten fell to the
roof on its feet, and made its
way carefully down to the
kitchen, where the housekeeper
took off the dolls' clothes in
much astonishment.

Amelia didn't fall on her
feet, because she wasn't a
cat but a doll! She slid
down the roof. She
hung for a moment in
the gutter. She fell
over the gutter –
down, down, down
– and into the
prickly holly bush
that grew just
below!

'Ooh-ee-ow-ee-oh!' yelled Amelia,
for the holly bush pricked her well!
She scrambled out somehow and after
a long time got back to the nursery.

But when she crept in at the door,
what a fright she gave the toys! She
was covered in soot from head to toe.
Her clothes were all torn! Her face
and arms were pricked and scratched!

'Oooooh!' yelled the toys and
rushed to shut themselves in the
cupboard. 'What is it? What is it?'

'It's me, Amelia Jane,' said Amelia,
in a very small voice. 'I've come back.'

'Well, you look DREADFUL!' said
Teddy, sticking his head out of the
cupboard. 'For goodness' sake
undress and have a bath and put on

clean clothes!'

So Amelia did – but the clothes in
the dolls' chest were much too small
for her, and she did look funny
walking about in things belonging to
the baby doll!

'I shall be good in future,' said
Amelia Jane. But I don't believe it, do
you?

Amelia Jane
and the soap

Amelia Jane was feeling very bored. She had behaved herself for a whole week!

'But only because she hasn't been able to think of anything naughty to do,' said Tom to Teddy. 'As soon as she thinks of something she'll cheer up and be as bad as ever.'

Well, it wasn't long before Amelia

Jane did cheer up. She had thought of something.

You see, it was like this – she had gone out for a nice walk, sitting in the dolls' pram, and she had been taken into the town. Now, racing up and down the pavement were two boys on roller-skates. What a pace they went!

Amelia Jane leaned out of the pram to watch them. She thought it was a lovely game. She tried to see what the boys had on their feet, but they went so fast that Amelia Jane really didn't see what the skates were like.

How *do* they slip along so fast? she thought. I *would* like to skate like that. How I wish I could! I'd go round and round the nursery, and down the passage and back. My, wouldn't the toys stare!

Now, when Amelia Jane had an idea she just had to carry it out. So when she got back to the nursery she sat at the back of the toy-cupboard and thought hard.

'I want to skate,' she said to herself. 'I want to put something on my feet and slip along like those boys. I want to go fast! But what can I put on my feet?'

'What are you thinking so hard about?' asked the clockwork clown, poking his head in at the door.

'Never you mind,' said Amelia Jane.

'Tell me, and maybe I can help,' said the clown.

'Well, I'm trying to think of something nice and slippery,' said Amelia Jane.

'What about jelly?' said the clown.

'Don't be silly,' said Amelia.

'Well, soap,' said the clown. 'Nice wet soap! Why, the other day I got hold of some wet soap and squeezed it – and it shot out of my hand like lightning and hit Tom on the ear!'

Amelia Jane laughed. Then she

stopped and thought quickly. Soap!
Yes – that was really a *good* idea! If
she got two nice pieces of soap, made
them wet and slippery and tied them
under her feet, she would be able to
slip along just like those boys on
skates! Good!

'I'll try it!' said Amelia Jane. So
she ran out of the toy-cupboard and
went to the nursery basin. She
climbed up and looked to see if there

was any soap there. There was – and what luck! – it had broken into two nice pieces.

'Oooh!' said Amelia, in delight. 'Just what I want!'

She turned on the tap and wetted the soap till it was so slippery she could hardly hold it. Then she climbed down with it. The toys looked at her in amazement.

'What are you going to do?' said

Teddy. 'Are you going to give yourself a good wash for once?'

'Don't be rude,' said Amelia. 'You'll see in a minute what I'm going to do.'

She took off a hair-ribbon and tore it in two. Naughty Amelia! Then she tied one piece of soap under her right foot and the other piece under her left foot. The toys stared at her as if they thought she was mad.

'Amelia, that's a funny way of washing your feet,' said Tom at last.

'I'm not washing my feet. I'm

going to *skate*!' said Amelia proudly.
'Turn back the carpet, somebody. I
must skate on the polished floor.'

The toys began to giggle. Really,
what *would* Amelia Jane do next!
Teddy and Tom turned back the
carpet. Unfortunately they rolled the
clockwork mouse up in it and had to
unroll it again to get him out.

'Oh, do be quick!' said Amelia
impatiently. 'I am simply longing to
begin!'

At last the carpet was rolled right
back. Amelia Jane began. She put
first one foot out – slid along a little
way on the soap – then put the other
foot forward and slid too – and before
the toys knew what she was about,

there she was, skating round the nursery on her soap-skates!

How the toys laughed! Really, it was too funny to see Amelia sliding along so fast on pieces of soap!

Amelia Jane tried to stop – but she toppled and fell over, bang! The toys roared. It was funny to watch Amelia sitting down, plop, glaring at them angrily.

'How dare you laugh at me!' cried Amelia Jane. 'I shall go and learn how to skate in the passage. There is a nice polished floor there – I shall slide beautifully!'

'No, stay here,' said the clown, in alarm. 'You know quite well that somebody may go along that passage and see you, Amelia Jane.'

'Pooh, everyone's in bed,' said Amelia, and this was true, for it was past midnight. 'Anyway, you won't be able to laugh at me there, if I fall down – for none of you dares to come into the passage.'

It was dark in the passage, for only a small light burnt there. Amelia slid out on her soap-skates and began to slide gaily up and down, up and down! The kitchen cat, hearing the noise, came creeping up the stairs, wondering if there was an extra-large-size mouse anywhere about.

He *was* astonished when he saw Amelia. He ran along the passage to see what she had on her feet. Amelia

didn't hear him or see him, and she
suddenly bumped right into him.
Crash! She fell over and banged her

head against the bedroom door.

'Sh! Amelia Jane! Sh!' whispered
Tom, putting his head out of the
nursery door. But Amelia Jane

wouldn't hush. She got up angrily and shooed the cat away. But the cat spat and hissed, which scared her a bit.

If Amelia Jane had been sensible she would have run back to the nursery at once, but she was so keen on skating that she once more began to slide up and down, up and down, all along the passage. She didn't hear Nanny's bed creaking. She didn't hear Nanny creeping to the door. She didn't even see Nanny poking her head round the door – no, she went slipping and sliding up and down on the soap, having a perfectly lovely time!

Nanny couldn't make out who or what it was, for the passage was so dark. But she could quite well see something going up and down the passage, skating quickly. She moved to the light switch to put a brighter light on.

Amelia Jane saw her then. Quick as lightning the doll slipped through the nursery door, fell over on the carpet, tore off the bits of soap, and ran to the toy-cupboard. She climbed in on top of the bear and the clown, who were very angry at being walked on.

But nobody dared to say a word! Suppose Nanny had seen what was happening? But when Nanny turned on the big light, all she saw was the kitchen cat sitting calmly by the wall.

'Good gracious,' she said, 'so it was *you* I saw, Puss, skating up and down the passage! What do you mean by doing that in the middle of the night, I should like to know! My goodness, what is the world coming to, when cats take to sliding up and down passages and waking everybody up! Shoo! Shoo!'

She shooed the cat down the stairs, and he disappeared quickly, tail in air, boiling with rage to think that Amelia Jane had slipped off and left him to take the blame.

And in the morning, when Nanny saw the messy bits of soap lying on the carpet, she was crosser than ever.

'Just look at that!' she said to Jane,

the cleaner. 'It must be that cat. Slipped and slid down the passage all night long like a mad thing – and then went and tried to eat the soap out of the basin!'

Poor Puss got a scolding! Amelia Jane laughed at him – but she didn't laugh quite so much when the cat came downstairs and tore her new dress with his sharp claws.

'You'd better not skate any more with the soap, Amelia Jane,' said Tom. 'It's funny to watch you – but if you get other people into trouble it's not fair!'

So that was the end of Amelia Jane skating on the soap. I would have loved to see her, wouldn't you?

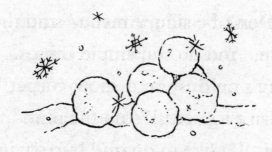

Amelia Jane and the Snow

It was snowing hard. The toys looked out of the nursery window and watched the big white snowflakes come floating down.

'The garden has a new white carpet,' said the teddy bear.

'Let's send the clockwork clown out to sweep the dust off it!' said Amelia Jane, the big naughty doll, with a giggle.

'Don't be silly, Amelia,' said the clown. 'You do say stupid things. There's no dust on a snow-carpet!'

'Isn't it pretty!' said the pink rabbit. 'I'd like to go and burrow in it!'

'Let's go and play in it!' said the golden-haired doll. 'It would be such fun.'

'Come on, then!' said Amelia

Jane. She ran to the door, peeped out, and beckoned the others. 'Nobody's about. We'll slip out of the garden door and go to the bit of garden behind the hedge. Nobody will see us there.'

'Stop a bit, Amelia Jane,' said the clockwork clown. 'Put on a coat. It's very cold outside.'

'Pooh!' said Amelia impatiently. 'Don't be such a baby, Clockwork Clown! I shall be as warm as toast running about. I'm going!'

She ran off down the stairs. But the other toys stayed to put on hats, coats, and scarves. Even the clockwork mouse put a red handkerchief round his neck.

When they got out to the snow they found that Amelia Jane had already made herself a great many snowballs! She danced about as they came, and shouted in glee.

'Let's have a snow-fight! Come on! I've got my snowballs ready. Look out, clown! Look out, pink rabbit!'

The big doll threw a snowball hard. It hit the clown on the head and he fell over, plonk! Amelia Jane giggled. She threw a snowball at the golden-haired doll and hit her in her middle. The doll gave a squeal and sat down in the snow.

'Ooh, this is fun!'

yelled Amelia. 'Come on, everyone, get some snowballs ready!'

But nobody could make such big hard snowballs as Amelia Jane. Amelia did enjoy herself. She pelted all the toys with snowballs, hitting them on the head and the chest and the legs – anywhere she could. She was quite a good shot, and the toys got very angry.

'Amelia Jane! Stop!' shouted Tom. 'It isn't fair. Your snowballs are three times as big as ours, and you make

them so hard that they hurt. Stop, I tell you!'

But Amelia

Jane wouldn't stop. No, she went on and on – and how she laughed when all the toys turned and ran away from her shower of snowballs!

'Let's leave her alone,' said the clown crossly. 'She's too tiresome for anything.'

'But she'll follow us and go on snowballing us,' said the mouse.

'No, she won't. She's found something else to snowball,' said the teddy bear. 'Look! She's snowballing the kitten!'

So she was. The kitten didn't mind the snowballs at all because she could always dodge them. She pounced on them as they fell, and Amelia Jane laughed to see her. She forgot about the toys.

'What shall we do?' said the golden-haired doll.

'Let's build a nice, round snow-house,' said the clown eagerly. 'It would be such fun to do that. I know how to. You just pile nice hard snow round in a ring and gradually make a round wall higher and higher. Then you make the wall slope inwards till the sides meet, and that's the roof!'

'Oh yes, that would be lovely!' said Tom. 'We could all live in the snow-house then.'

'But we won't let Amelia Jane come in at all,' said the clockwork mouse, getting a little snowball for the wall of the house.

'No, we won't,' said the golden-haired doll. 'It will punish her for throwing such hard snowballs at us.'

The toys worked hard at their snow-house. Soon the wall was quite high. It was a perfectly round wall. It grew higher and higher – and at last, as the toys shaped it to go inwards, the round sides met together and made a rounded roof.

The toys made a dear little doorway at the bottom. They were very excited, for the house was lovely. The clown ran to the pond, cut a square piece of ice, and ran back with it.

'What's that for?' asked the pink
rabbit.

'A window, of course!' said the

clown. He made a square hole in the
side of the house and fitted in the
piece of ice. It made a lovely window!

'Now let's go inside and be cosy,' said the golden-haired doll. So they all crowded into the dear little snow-house and sat down. It was lovely.

But just as the clockwork clown was telling a nice story, Amelia Jane came up. The kitten had gone indoors, and Amelia Jane wanted someone else to play with. She had looked and looked for the toys, but as they were in the snow-house she hadn't seen them.

She suddenly saw the house and came running up to it. She peeped inside the window.

'Oh, what a nice little house!' she cried. 'Let me come in, too!'

'No, Amelia Jane!' shouted all the

toys. 'You are too big. Besides, we don't want you.'

'But I'm very, very cold,' said Amelia Jane, and certainly she was shivering.

'Well, you should have been sensible and put on your coat and hat as we did!' said the golden-haired doll.

'Oh, *do* let me come in!' begged Amelia, who hated to be left out of anything. 'Oh, do let me!'

'NO, NO, NO!' shouted the toys.

'Well, I'm *coming* in!' said Amelia crossly, and she began to push her way in at the door. A bit of the doorway fell down at once.

'Don't!' cried the clown, in alarm. 'You will break our house!'

'Serve you right!' said naughty Amelia. But the toys really couldn't bear to see their house broken.

'All right, all right, you can come in,' said Tom. 'But wait till we get out, Amelia. You are so big that there isn't room for anyone else when *you're* inside!'

That pleased Amelia very much. She thought it would be lovely to have the house all to herself. She waited until all the toys had squeezed out of the house, and then she went in.

'Oh, it's lovely!' she cried. She pressed her nose to the window and looked out. 'It's lovely! It's a real little house. This shall be mine. You build another one for yourselves, Toys.'

But the toys were tired. They stared angrily at Amelia Jane.

'You are a very naughty, selfish doll,' shouted the teddy bear. 'First you snowball us till we have to run away. Then you take our house for your own.'

'I'm cold,' said the clown, shivering. 'Let's go and slide on the ice for a bit. Perhaps Amelia will get tired of our house soon and we can have it again.'

So they went off to the pond and left Amelia Jane by herself.

Amelia felt cold. She shivered and shook in the little snow-house. 'I wish there was a fire in this house,' she said to herself, 'then it would be nice and warm. I'll make one! How the toys will stare when they see I have a nice fire to warm myself by! But I shan't let them come in at all!'

She ran to the wood-shed and got some wood. She found some matches there that the gardener used when he lit a bonfire. She ran back to the snow-house. Soon the twigs were crackling loudly.

'What's that noise?' said the clown suddenly. All the toys stopped their sliding and listened. It came from their snow-house.

'Amelia Jane is lighting a fire there!' said Tom. Then the toys looked at one another – and began to giggle. They knew quite well what would happen if anyone lit a fire in a house made of snow! They ran up to watch.

'You can't come in, you can't come in!' shouted Amelia Jane. 'This is my house, and this is my own dear little warm fire! Oh, I'm so cosy! Oh, I'm so warm!'

The toys stood and watched. The fire blazed up as the twigs burnt.

There was a red glow inside the little house. It certainly looked very cosy. Amelia Jane put out her hands and warmed them inside the house.

But something was happening. The fire was melting the house! After all, it was only made of snow! The walls began to drip. The roof began to drip. The bit of ice that was the window disappeared altogether.

Amelia Jane felt the drips on her back and was cross.

'Who's pouring water on me?' she cried. 'Stop it, or I'll be very angry!'

Drip, drip, drip went the snow as it melted all around her. And suddenly the whole house fell in, for the snow was now so soft and melty that it

couldn't hold together. The fire went
out with a sizzle.

Amelia Jane disappeared, for the
snow fell all over her!

'Oooh! Ow! What's happened?'
yelled Amelia Jane, very frightened.

She kicked about in the wet snow, and first her hands came out, and then her head. She sat in the snow and looked around.

'Ha ha! Ho ho ho!' roared the toys. 'It serves you right, Amelia Jane! You took our house – and you lit a fire and melted it – and it fell on top of you! Ha ha! Ho ho ho!'

Amelia Jane began to cry. She was wet through and very cold. She ran back to the nursery, leaving little wet marks all the way. She sat by the fire there and tried to get dry.

And very soon she began to sneeze: 'A-tishooo! A-tishoo!'

'Now I've got a cold!' she said miserably. 'Oh, why do I get naughty? Something nasty always happens to me when I do!'

'Well, just try and remember that, next time you feel naughty,' said Tom, giving Amelia his big red handkerchief.

But I don't expect she'll remember it, do you?

Amelia Jane Goes Mad

Once, when Amelia Jane, that big rascal of a doll, had been good for simply ages, she suddenly got tired of it and went quite mad! Never in her life had she been so naughty and, really, the toys got quite scared of her!

She was quite silly over water. She thought it was the greatest fun to fill the watering-can that belonged to the children, and lie in wait for any toy to come by at night.

She hid behind the curtain and waited till Tom came by. Then she tilted up the little green can and watered him! Goodness, how he jumped!

'It's raining!' he cried, and ran to get his umbrella. But when he put it up, no rain fell at all, and everyone laughed at him.

'It never rains in the nursery, silly!' said the clockwork clown.

'Well, look at my wet hair,' said

Tom, and he shook a shower of drops all over the clown. 'What do you call that if it isn't rain?'

The clockwork clown snorted, and went to visit the clockwork mouse over in the corner. He didn't know that Amelia Jane was hiding behind the scuttle with the watering-can again! Just as he came by, whistling a merry little tune, Amelia tilted up the can – and, pitter-patter! down came the water over the startled clown.

He ran to get the umbrella then – and holding it carefully over him, he went back to the scuttle to find out what the water was. And there, of course, he found Amelia, laughing till the tears ran down her cheeks.

'Give me that watering-can, Amelia Jane,' said the clockwork clown sternly. When he spoke like that, he had to be obeyed, so Amelia meekly gave him the can. But she soon began to look around for some more water to play with.

This time she found a very naughty thing to do. She found that if she stood on a chair by the wash-basin and turned on the tap, she could make the water spurt out all over the room by putting her hand under the tap. And she waited till the golden-haired doll came by, and then spurted the water all over her!

The golden-haired doll was angry, because the water went on her hair and took out the curl. So she was a straight-haired doll then, and everyone thought she looked most peculiar.

'I shall have to put my hair in curl-papers tonight, and they are so uncomfortable,' sighed the doll. 'Oh, how I wish I could *punish* Amelia Jane!'

Well, the clown climbed up to the basin, and with his strong hands he turned off the two taps so very tightly that not even Amelia Jane could turn them on again. So she couldn't play *that* trick any more.

Never mind! thought Amelia. I shall think of something else! What fun it is to play with water!

Well, she just couldn't get any water from the taps, and the toys felt safe. But Amelia Jane knew somewhere else to get water. Yes – the goldfish bowl was full of water for the two goldfish to swim in!

The goldfish lived on a table by the wall. Amelia Jane climbed up to the wash-basin and took the sponge from there. It was quite dry. Then she climbed up to the goldfish bowl and looked into the water.

'Can I borrow some of your water?' she asked the fish. And then, without waiting for an answer, she dipped the sponge into the water and made it dripping wet.

Amelia sat on the table and

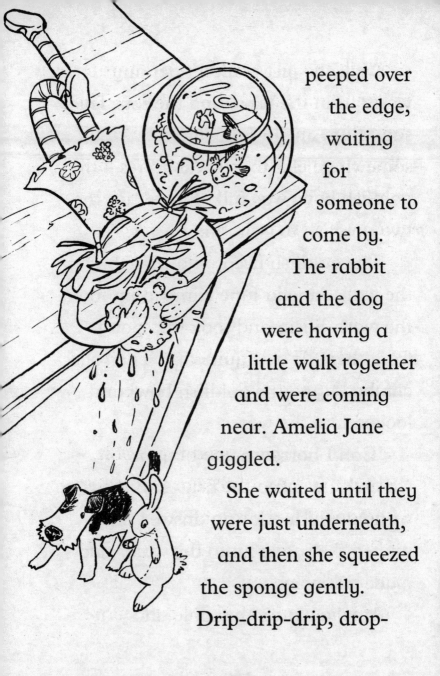

peeped over
the edge,
waiting
for
someone to
come by.
The rabbit
and the dog
were having a
little walk together
and were coming
near. Amelia Jane
giggled.
She waited until they
were just underneath,
and then she squeezed
the sponge gently.
Drip-drip-drip, drop-

drop-drop! Large cold drops of water fell on to the dog and the rabbit. They were most surprised. They looked up – but Amelia was no longer peeping over the edge of the table, and they could see nothing. They couldn't understand it.

'I'm wet,' said the rabbit, shaking himself.

'And I'm wet too,' said the dog, licking himself. 'Where did it come from?'

'Can't imagine,' said the rabbit. 'Perhaps we are mistaken. Come, let us go on with our ramble.'

So on they went again, and Amelia Jane watched for them to come back near the table once more.

Just as they passed, she held out her sponge and squeezed it hard again.

Drip-drip-drip, drop-drop-drop! Down came the water and soaked the dog and the rabbit. How angry they were!

'My ears are dripping,' said the rabbit.

'My whiskers are soaked,' said the dog. 'Let us tell the clown.'

Well, as soon as they complained to the clown, he knew quite well it must be Amelia Jane up to her water-tricks again, and he called to her very sternly:

'Amelia Jane! Will you stop soaking everyone? It isn't funny, it is very silly, for you will give everyone a dreadful cold. Where are you?'

But Amelia Jane wouldn't answer, though she was aching with trying to stop laughing. The clown was angry, and set out to look for her. He came too near the table and Amelia Jane saw him.

'I can't help it!' she said to herself. 'I must throw this nice wet sponge at him!'

So she threw the sponge at the clown, and it hit him full in the middle. He fell down with a thud, and the sponge dripped wet on him from top to toe. He got up and stared angrily round. But he could *not* see Amelia Jane. She was crouching down on the top of the table again, behind the goldfish bowl.

The clown went to talk to the doll, whose hair was now in curl-papers. The rabbit, the dog, Tom, and the clockwork mouse came too.

'It's time we stopped Amelia Jane,' said the clown. 'What about doing something to *her* with water? That would really be a good punishment!'

'But how can we?' asked the doll with curl-papers. 'If we throw the sponge at her, she'll only throw it back. And you've hidden the can so that she can't get it.'

Everybody thought hard. And then the clockwork mouse had an idea! He was only a small toy, but he sometimes had surprisingly big ideas.

'I know!' he said. 'What about a siphon of soda-water?'

All the toys stared at him as if he were quite mad. '*You* know!' said the mouse. 'The thing that the big people keep in the dining-room, and squirt into a glass when they want a drink. I've seen them. What about getting one of those out of the kitchen where they are stored, and having a squirt at Amelia Jane? If she's so fond of water, she might like a bit of squirting!'

The toys laughed. The clockwork clown and the rabbit went out of the nursery and down the passage to the kitchen to see if they could find a siphon. They found one quite easily in the larder. It was terribly heavy. They had to fetch the dog to help them to carry it back to the nursery.

Amelia Jane had got down from the table and was busy tying a new hair-ribbon in her yellow hair. She was surprised to hear the heavy bumping as the toys carried the siphon in at the door. She turned round and laughed.

'Whatever have you brought that great ugly thing for?' she asked.

'Do you want to know?' said the clown, bringing it right up to her. Before she could answer, the toys pressed on the handle of the siphon, and the soda-water squirted out with a tremendous hissing noise, right into

Amelia Jane's surprised face!

Good gracious! She was so startled that she fell over! The toys squealed with delight and squirted her on the ground. She got up and ran away in a dreadful fright. But the toys followed her, and squirted her all the way! Oh dear, oh dear! Poor Amelia, what a shock she got! The siphon made such a noise, and the water soaked her and ran down her neck and quite took her breath away!

'Do you like water so much now?' cried the clown. 'Do you think it is nice to be soaked? Squirt-squirt-squirt! How do you like to be watered, Amelia Jane?'

Well, Amelia certainly did *not* like it! She squealed and screamed and made such a noise that the toys were really afraid she would wake up everyone who was asleep. So they stopped squirting her and quietly took the siphon back to the kitchen.

Poor Amelia Jane! She had to take off all her clothes, even her underwear, and dry them by the fire. Even her body was wet, and she had to dry that too, turning herself round and round all night long! I don't think she will play with water again, somehow!

And nobody in the house could think where all the soda-water out of that siphon had gone to. Amelia Jane isn't likely to tell them, anyhow!

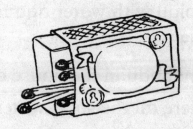

Amelia Jane and the Matches

This is the tale of Amelia Jane and the matches.

Now all boys and girls, unless they are quite old, are warned by their fathers and mothers never to play with matches. And with toys it is just the same. They must never play with matches, in case they get on fire and burn themselves.

But you can guess that Amelia Jane didn't care about any danger! No! If she could get hold of matches you may be sure she would!

There were never any matches left in the nursery, till one day when Jane lit the fire and forgot to put the matches back in her apron pocket, as she usually did.

Jane left the box of matches on the mantelpiece and Amelia Jane saw it first, of course because she was quite the tallest toy in the nursery.

'Oooh!' she said, pointing upwards. 'Matches! If only I could get them!'

'Don't be naughty,' said the clockwork clown at once. 'You know that children and toys must never touch matches.'

'Pooh!' said Amelia Jane rudely.

'Don't pooh at me like that!' said the clockwork clown. 'It's rude.'

'Pooh, pooh, pooh!' said Amelia Jane. So you can guess she was in one of her naughty moods again.

She stood and thought for a minute. Then she remembered how the cowboy doll had taught her to throw a lasso round anything and jerk it near. If only she could make a loop of rope and throw it carefully, she could get those matches down easily.

She ran to the string-box and opened it. The teddy bear saw her. 'If you're thinking of lassoing those matches and getting them down, just let me remind you what happened last time you tried your hand at that!' he said. 'You lassoed the bowl of tadpoles, and got them all down your neck.'

Amelia Jane took no notice. She got out a long piece of string and made a loop-knot at the end. Then she stood beneath the mantelpiece and threw the string neatly upwards, holding one end in her hand.

'Ooooh!' said all the toys in surprise, because, will you believe it, Amelia Jane got the loop right round the box, and it fell almost at her feet when she pulled the string!

'Aren't I clever!' said Amelia proudly.

'No, you're not, you're just lucky,' said the clockwork clown. 'You're not to touch those matches, Amelia Jane.'

'Pooh!' said Amelia, and she opened the box. 'Now, who wants to see me strike a match?'

The toys felt frightened. They knew quite well that matches can set fire to things and burn them. They ran to the toy-cupboard and crept inside, all except the clockwork mouse, and he did badly want to see a match struck.

'I'd like to see some matches struck, please, Amelia,' he said, and he ran nearer.

'Well, you shall see a whole lot struck!' said the big doll. 'The others have all run away, the sillies. You and I will enjoy ourselves!'

Amelia opened the box. She took out a match. She struck it hard on the side of the box. Fizzz-zzz-zzz! The match lit and Amelia Jane held it up in the air, watching the bright flame.

The clockwork mouse liked it very much indeed. He thought it was most exciting.

'Please, please, let me light one too,' he begged.

'Amelia Jane, if you let the mouse strike a match we'll all come out of the cupboard and punish you,' shouted the clockwork clown. 'He's too little to do dangerous things like that.'

'All right, all right!' said Amelia, striking another match. 'I shan't let him. Besides, I want to strike them all myself!'

But before Amelia Jane could strike any more matches there came the sound of steps on the landing outside. The toys flopped down. Amelia ran to the cupboard, throwing the box of matches into a corner. The clockwork mouse ran into the brick-box. So when

Jane looked into the nursery, there was no one to be seen at all. Everything was quiet. She had come to put some fresh flowers on the table. Then she dusted round a bit and went downstairs again.

The toys didn't come out for a long time – not until it was night, for they were afraid of being caught. The first toy that came alive was the clockwork mouse. He saw the box of matches in the corner and was pleased. He ran to them and pushed them along with his nose till he came to a slipper. He popped them into the slipper.

Aha! he thought. Now no one will know where they are, and I can strike as many as I like when the others are not looking!

Now when all the toys came out of the cupboard they looked very stern indeed. They were angry with Amelia Jane. She had no right to teach the clockwork mouse to play with matches!

The toys sat round Amelia in a circle, and scolded her.

'We shall none of us talk to you for a week,' said the teddy bear.

'We shall not play with you at all,' said the clockwork clown.

'You will not have any of the sweets out of the toy sweet-shop,' said the golden-haired doll.

'And we have hidden your fine new bonnet so that you can't wear it when you go out,' said the pink rabbit.

'Pooh!' said Amelia Jane – but not in a very poohy voice. She was upset. She hated not being talked to or played with. It would be horrid not to have any sweets. And oh, fancy hiding her lovely new bonnet so that she couldn't wear it! Amelia Jane felt like crying. She walked over to the window-seat and sat there, sniffing hard. She was very unhappy.

Suddenly the toys heard a curious noise.

Fizz-zz-zz-zz!

It was the clockwork mouse

striking a match all by himself. The toys stared at him in horror. He struck another and squeaked in delight.

But oh, my goodness me, what do you think happened?' His whiskers caught alight! Yes, they really did, and the poor little mouse found himself on fire, with flames burning each side of his little face!

'Sizzle-sizzle!' went his fine whiskers. The mouse squealed in fright and flung away the lighted match. Oh dear – it fell on to an open book and the pages caught alight! The book flamed up, and set light to the brick-box nearby.

'Crackle-crackle!' went the flames merrily. 'Crackle-crackle! We're going

to eat the book! We're going to eat the
brick-box! Then we'll eat the carpet –
and the chairs – and the toy-
cupboard – and all the toys – and the
whole house! Crackle, crackle,
crackle!'

It was dreadful. The toys stared in
horror and couldn't move even a paw,
they were so frightened. No wonder
they had been warned against
playing with matches. This was what
happened when they disobeyed!

'Eee-eee-eee!' squealed the poor
little clockwork mouse, his whiskers
burning all away. He ran to and fro
in pain and fright. All the toys
watched and trembled dreadfully.

And what about that big, naughty

doll, Amelia Jane? Yes – she was watching too, her face pale with fright. Poor, poor little mouse – how she wished she hadn't shown him how to strike matches! And oh, that book – and the lovely brick-box! Whatever would happen to them all?

'Well, I began it, so I must try and stop it!' cried Amelia Jane. 'I remember hearing someone say that if anyone got on fire they should be rolled round tightly in a rug to put the flames out. Where, oh, where is a rug?'

'In the dolls' pram!' yelled the teddy bear, who was still too frightened to move.

Amelia Jane ran to the dolls' pram.

She snatched up the thick blue rug there and rushed to the little clockwork mouse. She threw the rug all round his little grey body and rolled him up tightly in it, head, tail, and all! She felt the flames trying to burn her hands, and they hurt her, but she didn't stop. She meant to save the little mouse!

The thick rug squashed all the flames out. They died away. There were none left. The clockwork mouse wasn't on fire any more.

But the book and the brick-box were still burning away. Amelia Jane left the mouse and ran to the basin with a jug. She stood on a chair, turned on the tap and filled the jug. Down she climbed and rushed to the brick-box. She threw the water over the flames.

'Sizzle-sizzle!' they said, and died out. They could not go on burning when water was thrown over them. Then Amelia fetched another jug of water and threw it over the burning book.

'Sizzle-sizzle!' said the flames again, and went out. The fire was gone!

The toys came round, looking quite pale. Amelia Jane sat down and began to cry.

'I wish I hadn't touched the matches, I wish I hadn't!' she sobbed.

'I've got no whiskers now!' wept the poor little clockwork mouse. Sure enough, he hadn't – and he did look funny without them. What a noise Amelia Jane and the mouse made, sobbing together!

'You'll never speak to me or play with me again,' wept Amelia, looking round at the toys. 'I might as well go away from here and never come back.'

'Now listen, Amelia Jane,' said the teddy bear, putting his arm round her. 'You did a very wrong thing, and it has caused a lot of damage – but you have done your best to put it right, and you were brave when all of us were too afraid to do anything.'

'So we will have to forgive you,' said the clown. 'We were angry with you when you were bad, but we think you are brave too, so cheer up.'

'What about the mouse's whiskers, though – and the burnt book and brick-box?' wept Amelia.

'The mouse will have to do without his whiskers,' said Tom. 'The book was very old and torn, so perhaps it won't matter being burnt; and as for the brick-box, it's only the lid that has been burnt, and I can make a new one with the carpenter's set in the toy cupboard. But look at your own hands – and the front of your dress! They are burnt too!'

'It serves me right,' said Amelia

Jane. 'I'll put some good ointment on my hands, and I'll have to go about with a burnt bit of dress in front. Oh, I'm so glad you've forgiven me, Toys! I won't be naughty again.'

Well, the toys didn't believe *that*, of course – they knew Amelia Jane too well! But they were soon good friends again, and, secretly, they couldn't help admiring Amelia Jane for putting out the fire so quickly, and saving the little mouse.

'She's like the little girl in the nursery rhyme,' said the bear to the clown. '*You* know – when she's good she's *very, very* good – but when she's bad she's horrid!'

Enid Blyton™

Amelia Jane
Gets Into Trouble!

EGMONT

Contents

Amelia Jane and the Telephone

There was a new toy in the nursery. It was a little telephone. It stood on the nursery book-shelf looking exactly like a real one, but much smaller.

The toys didn't dare to touch it. They were afraid of the real telephone, and they were afraid of the toy one, too.

Outside in the passage they often heard the bell of the real telephone ringing loudly, and it made them jump. Then someone would come along, take the receiver off the telephone and speak into it.

'Hallo!' they would say. 'Hallo!' And then they would speak to somebody far, far away, and it all seemed very like magic.

Amelia Jane, the big naughty doll, had been away for a few days. When she came back the first thing she saw was the toy telephone.

'Aha!' she said, and went over to it. 'A telephone. Good. We need one in the nursery.'

'Don't touch it, Amelia Jane – a telephone is very magic,' cried Tom the toy soldier. 'Voices come into it, you know – people who are far, far away can speak to you. Be careful, in case somebody's voice is in that toy telephone now!'

'Pooh!' said Amelia Jane. 'I'm just going to do a bit of ordering – like Mother does sometimes on the real telephone out in the passage.'

And, to the toys' horror, she picked up the little receiver, put one end to her ear, and spoke into the other end.

'Is that the butcher? Send four sausages to the nursery, please. Is that the baker? Send four buns to the nursery, please. Is that the watchmaker? Send one nice new watch to the nursery, please – and, oh, please see that the letters

A. J. are on the back. A. J. for Amelia Jane. Thank you.' She put back the receiver and smiled round at the astonished toys. 'There you are! I've done a nice little bit of ordering. We'll enjoy the sausages and the buns. We can divide them up between us. And I always wanted a watch.'

Of course, Amelia Jane knew quite well that she hadn't been speaking to the butcher, the baker and the watchmaker. She was just making the toys think she was very daring and grand.

But the toys were really very worried. They climbed up to the window-sill to watch for the goods to arrive.

'The thing is – how are we to pay for them?' said the teddy bear. 'I haven't got any money!'

'I've got a penny that I found under the carpet,' said the clockwork mouse.

'Shall we be put into prison if we order things we can't pay for?' asked the clockwork clown.

Nobody knew – but they thought it was very likely. Tom the toy soldier went to Amelia Jane.

'Please, Amelia Jane, ring up the butcher, the baker and the watchmaker and tell them not to send the things after all,' he said.

'What will you give me if I do?' asked Amelia Jane at once.

'Oh dear – I'll give you my best hanky,' said Tom. 'And the mouse will give you his penny. Have *you* got anything to give, Teddy?'

'Just a good scolding,' said the teddy, rather fiercely. 'I'll give that with pleasure.'

'Give me the hanky and the money, and I'll ring up the butcher, the baker and the watchmaker,' said Amelia Jane. So they gave her them, and she went to the telephone.

'I haven't given you my scolding,' said the bear, but Amelia took no notice. She spoke into the telephone:

'Is that the butcher? We don't want the sausages after all. Is that the baker? We don't want the buns. Is that the watchmaker? I've changed my mind about the watch. Yes – yes. That's right. What's that? You want to send a message to the teddy bear? Oh, yes, of course, I'll give it to him.'

The toys were listening with all

their ears. 'Right,' said Amelia, into the telephone. 'I'm to tell the bear he is a nasty, fat, tubby little creature, who can't even growl like a bear. Yes, certainly I'll tell him!'

'Don't you dare to tell me,' said the bear fiercely.

'All right, Teddy, I won't tell you that you are a nasty, fat, tubby little creature who can't even growl like a bear,' said Amelia Jane, annoyingly.

'But you *have* told him!' said Tom.

'No – I just told him what I wouldn't tell him,' said Amelia Jane.

She climbed up on to a shelf where nobody could reach her, not even the bear. She thought about the toy telephone. It would be very very useful, she could see that. She would be able to make up all kinds of rude messages to pass on to the toys. She began to make a little plan.

Yes – she would invent somebody at the other end – somebody who would keep ringing up – and she would pretend to answer the telephone, and then give the horrid messages to all the toys. That would keep them in order all right!

She slipped down and went to the small toy bicycle that stood at one end of the nursery. It had a tiny little bell. She unscrewed it and put it into her pocket. She could ring it whenever she wanted to – and

she would pretend it was the
telephone bell ringing. That would
make the toys jump!

The toys made up a song about
Amelia Jane.

Amelia Jane
Is naughty again,
Let's go and leave her
Out in the rain.
Nobody loves her,
Nobody cares
If she gets eaten
By lions or bears.
She wants a scolding,
It's perfectly plain;
Amelia Jane,
You are naughty again!

Amelia listened to this song and
felt very angry indeed. How dare they
sing that? Why, even the clockwork

mouse was singing and waving his tail about in time to the tune. Amelia walked over to the telephone and sat down by it.

She put her hand into her pocket and rang the little bell. It sounded just like the telephone bell suddenly ringing. The toys stopped singing in great surprise.

'The telephone rang!' they said to one another. 'Would you believe it? The telephone rang. Answer it, Amelia. See who wants to speak to us.'

Amelia picked up the receiver and put one end to her ear. 'Dear me – is that really Mr Mumbo-Jumbo?' she said, sounding astonished. 'This is Amelia Jane. What do you want, dear Mr Mumbo-Jumbo?'

The toys listened to this in amazement. Amelia Jane went on speaking. 'Yes, yes – I'll tell the bear. You're coming for him this evening, and you'll pull his nose for him till it's as long as an elephant's trunk. Yes, Mr Mumbo-Jumbo. Oh, yes – he is a bad bear. He deserves it. I'm sorry he was once so rude to you. Goodbye.'

She put down the receiver. The bear was trembling like a jelly, he was so scared.

'I was never rude to Mr Mumbo-Jumbo,' he wailed. 'I don't even know him. I never met him. I won't have my nose pulled, I won't, I won't.'

'I won't let you,' said Tom, comfortingly. 'I'll fight him.'

'So will I,' said the clockwork mouse, bravely. 'I'll nibble a hole in his leg.'

The telephone bell rang again –
though, of course, it was only Amelia
Jane putting her hand into her pocket
and ringing the little bicycle bell. She
picked up the receiver again and
spoke into it.

'Hallo! Who's that? Oh, Mr
Mumbo-Jumbo again – what do you
want this time, dear Mr Mumbo-

Jumbo? Yes, the clockwork mouse lives here – and the toy soldier too. No, they are not very nice toys. What am I to tell them? You are coming tonight to catch the toy soldier and peg him to your clothes-line? And you're going to peg the clockwork mouse up by his tail? Right, I'll tell them. Goodbye.'

'Oooooh!' squealed the clockwork mouse in fright. 'He's not to come! I never did him any harm!'

'Nor did I,' said Tom, turning pale. 'Who's this awful fellow? He's not to come. I've never been pegged up on a clothes-line in my life, and nobody's going to do that to me.'

The bell rang again and Amelia Jane once more spoke into the telephone. 'Oh – it's you, Mr Mumbo-Jumbo, again. What's that?

You'll scold any toy who is rude to me? Thank you very much indeed. I'll tell you tonight who you can scold very severely!'

She made a rude face at the listening toys and went over to her cot. She climbed in. 'I'm going to have a good sleep,' she said. 'And anyone who disturbs me will be reported to Mr Mumbo-Jumbo!'

She shut her eyes and was soon fast asleep. She turned in her sleep – and out of her pocket fell the little bicycle bell!

The clockwork clown pounced on it.

'Look at that! She rang this when she wanted us to think it was the telephone ringing! It was all a pretence on her part, the wicked doll.

There wasn't any Mr Mumbo-Jumbo speaking to her over the telephone!'

'Let's wake her,' said Tom fiercely.

'No,' said the clown, speaking in a whisper. 'I've got a better idea. I know where there's a long piece of rubber tubing. I'll get it and fix it to the ear-piece of the telephone – and then, whoever speaks at the other end of the rubber tube can be heard in the telephone – *really* heard, not just pretending.'

'What's the use of that?' asked the bear.

'Wait and see,' said the clown. 'Now tonight one of us will ring this little bell, as if the telephone was ringing again – and Amelia can go and answer it – and Tom shall speak through the tube . . .'

'Oooooh, yes,' said everyone. 'That's a fine idea!'

'And he shall say, in a very dreadful voice: "This is Mr Mumbo-Jumbo speaking. Is that Amelia Jane? I've heard what a bad doll you are. And I'm coming to get you, Amelia. I'm walking up the passage now – I'm banging at the door. Let me in!"'

'But – what's the good of that?' said the bear. 'He won't come walking up and banging at the door.'

'Yes, he will,' grinned the clown. 'I shall be outside, listening – and *I'll* come stamping up the passage, and *I'll* bang hard at the door – see?'

'Amelia will think it's really Mr Mumbo-Jumbo out there and she'll be scared out of her life!' said the bear, chuckling. 'What a fine idea. Where's the rubber tube, clown?'

Well, before Amelia woke up, the rubber tubing was fixed to the telephone and run secretly into the toy-cupboard, where Tom was hiding. They all waited till Amelia awoke and stepped out of the cot.

At the same moment the bear, who was by the telephone, rang the little bell that had fallen from Amelia's pocket. 'R-r-r-r-ring!'

Amelia jumped and looked surprised. But she walked over to the telephone and took off the receiver, meaning to make up some more messages from Mumbo-Jumbo. But to her astonishment and horror, a deep, hollow voice came to her ear.

'Is that Amelia Jane? This is Mr Mumbo-Jumbo speaking. I've heard

what a bad doll you are. And I'm
coming to get you, Amelia. I'm
walking up the passage now – I'm
BANGING at the door. Let me in!'

Amelia listened in fright. There
really *was* somebody speaking
through the telephone this time –
somebody who said he was *Mr
Mumbo-Jumbo*!

Then she heard the footsteps
stamping up the passage outside,
where the clown had hidden himself.
She heard the loud banging at the
door, and the shouts of 'Let me in!'

'No, no – don't let him in!' she
wailed, and she ran to the toy-
cupboard. 'Don't open the door, toys.
I'll be good. I'll never be bad again.
I'll give you back your hanky, Tom,
and your money, Mouse. Oh, oh,

don't let Mr Mumbo-Jumbo in.'

Bang-bang-BANG! 'Let me in,
I say!'

Amelia piled bricks all over herself
in the cupboard, trying to hide. Tom
went to the door of the nursery and
spoke sternly through it.

'Go away, Mr Mumbo-Jumbo.
We will let you know if Amelia Jane is
naughty again, and you can come
and get her then.'

And to Amelia's great relief she

heard footsteps stamping away from the door, and the banging stopped.

'Well, we've saved you from your friend, Mr Mumbo-Jumbo,' said Tom, looking into the cupboard. 'Are you going to behave yourself now, or not?'

'Oh, yes, yes,' sobbed Amelia Jane. 'Oh, that awful toy telephone. I'll never use it again.'

She didn't, of course. And, strange to say, neither did Mr Mumbo-Jumbo!

Now Then, Amelia Jane!

Amelia Jane, the big naughty doll in the nursery, was doing a bit of sewing. She sat in the corner, her head bent over her work, sewing away.

'Aha! So you've decided to sew on that shoe button at last!' said the clockwork clown, coming up. 'Quite time, too – your shoe's fallen off heaps of times!'

'You be quiet,' said Amelia Jane.

'And while you're about it, why not mend that hole in your dress?' said a wooden skittle, hopping up. 'Or do you *like* holes in your dress, Amelia Jane?'

'You be quiet, too,' said Amelia, and jabbed at him with her needle. He

hopped away with a chuckle.

He was soon back again. 'And what about your right stocking?' he said. 'It's got a great big hole in the heel. And what about . . . ?'

Amelia Jane jabbed at him again so hard that the thimble flew off her finger. It rolled away over the floor into a corner.

'Bother you, skittle!' said Amelia Jane, in a temper. 'Now you go and pick up that thimble and bring it back to me! Why do you tease me like this? I don't like you.'

'Shan't pick up your thimble!' said the skittle, enjoying himself. 'Silly old Amelia Jane!'

'Stop yelling at one another, and you go and pick up the thimble, skittle,' said the teddy bear, crossly.

'Can't you see I'm trying to read?'

The skittle didn't dare to disobey the big fat bear. He had once been rude to the bear and the bear had sat on him for a whole day, and the skittle hadn't liked that at all. The bear was so heavy.

So he picked up the thimble – but he didn't give it back to Amelia Jane. No – he put it on his head for a hat! Then he walked up and down in a very silly way, saying, 'Look at my new hat! Oh, *do* look at my new hat!'

Everybody looked, of course, and all the toys laughed at the skittle because he really did look funny in a thimble-hat.

He took it off and bowed to them, and then put it back again.

'*Will* you give me my thimble?' cried Amelia Jane, in a rage. 'Give it to me AT ONCE!'

'Say "please", Amelia,' said the bear. 'You sound very rude.'

'I *shan't* say "please"!' cried Amelia. 'And don't you interfere. Skittle, if you don't give me back my thimble at once I'll chase you and knock you over!'

'Can't catch *me*! Can't catch *me*!' said the skittle, who was really being very funny and very annoying. He ran here and there, and he kept taking his thimble-hat on and off to Amelia in a very ridiculous way.

Well, Amelia Jane wasn't going to

let a skittle be cheeky to her, so up she got. She raced after the skittle, and he rushed away. But Amelia Jane caught him – and do you know what she did? Instead of taking the thimble off his head, she pushed it so hard that it went right over the poor skittle's nose, and he couldn't see a thing.

'Oh! Oh, it's so tight now I can't get it off!' yelled the skittle, trying to force the thimble off his head.

Amelia Jane laughed.

'That'll teach you to wear my thimble for a hat and be so rude to me,' she said.

'Help, help!' shouted the skittle. 'It's hurting me! Oooooooooh! Ow! OOOOOOOOOOOH!'

'It really *is* hurting him,' said the bear, getting up. 'Dear, dear – I shall never finish my book today. Stand still, you silly skittle. I'll take the thimble off.'

Well, he tugged and he pulled, and he pulled and he tugged – but he couldn't get that thimble off!

Then Tom the toy soldier came up and had a try – but he couldn't get the thimble off either.

Amelia Jane tried – but it wasn't a

bit of good; that thimble was jammed so hard on the skittle's head that it really could *not* be moved!

'You'll have to wear the thimble always,' said the bear at last. The skittle lay down and yelled.

'I can't! I don't want to! Take it off, take it off! It's tight, I tell you!'

'We'll simply *have* to do something,' said Tom. 'Else the skittle will go on yelling for ever, and I don't think I could bear that.'

'Of *course* something must be done,' said the other skittles, who had popped up, looking very worried. 'Amelia Jane is very naughty.'

'That's nothing new,' said the bear. 'Dear me, do stop yelling, skittle. You'll wake up the household!'

Then the bear thought of

something. 'Oh, I've got an idea,' he said. 'What about going out to ask the little pixie who lives in the pansy bed if he knows of a spell to help us. A Get-Loose Spell, perhaps.'

'A good idea,' said Tom. 'Amelia Jane, go and find the pixie and ask him.'

'What! In the middle of a dark night!' said Amelia Jane. 'No, thank you. And anyway, I don't like that pixie!'

'Amelia Jane, if you don't go and ask him, we shall take your best ribbon and hide it,' said the bear.

'Oh, no, don't do that!' said Amelia. 'It's my party ribbon. All right, you horrid things – I'll go. But I know a very good way of getting the thimble off the skittle.'

'How?' asked the toys.

'Chop off his head!' said Amelia Jane. 'He has so few brains that he'd never even notice his head was gone!'

'We *will* take away your best ribbon now,' said the bear, as the skittle gave a loud yell of fright.

'No, no – I didn't mean it!' said Amelia Jane. 'I'll go this very minute to find the pixie.'

Well, off she went, climbing out of the window and down to the pansy bed.

The little pixie was there, wide awake.

'Pixie,' began Amelia, 'I want your help.'

'What will you give me for it?' asked the pixie, at once. He didn't like Amelia.

'Nothing,' said Amelia. 'Oh – let go of my foot, you horrid little pixie!'

'I'm taking your shoe for payment,' said the pixie. 'And the other one too. They will fit me nicely. Now, it's no good yelling. I've got them. I've no doubt you've been just as naughty as usual, so it serves you right. Now – what do you want my help for?'

Amelia Jane told him sulkily. 'The skittle is wearing my thimble jammed down hard on his head. How can we get it off?'

'Make the thimble bigger, of course,' said the pixie. 'Then his head will be too small for it and it will slip off.'

'But how can we make the thimble bigger?' asked Amelia Jane.

'Easy,' said the pixie. 'If you heat anything made of metal it becomes just a tiny bit larger – so heat the thimble, Amelia – and it will slip off the skittle's head.'

'But how can we heat it?' said Amelia, not really believing the pixie.

'Stand him on his head in hot water,' said the pixie. 'You could have thought of that yourself. Now go away. I want to try on your shoes.'

Amelia went back to the nursery. 'The pixie says that if we stand the skittle on his head in hot water, the thimble will get a bit larger and slip off,' said Amelia.

'I don't believe a word of it,' said the bear.

'Well, that's what he *said*,' said Amelia. 'He didn't tell me anything else. And I had to give him my shoes for that advice.'

'Hm,' said Tom. 'Well, poor old skittle – we'd better try it, anyway. Bear, put a little hot water into the basin, will you? Don't put the plug in in case it gets too deep – just let the water run in and out, and we'll pop the skittle in on his head, and heat the thimble in the water.'

Well, the skittle howled and yelled and kicked up a great fuss, but the bear and the toy soldier were very firm with him. They turned him upside down and held him in the hot water, so that the heat

warmed up the thimble on his head.

And will you believe it? – the thimble slipped off, just as the pixie had said it would. But alas – it rolled round the basin, and disappeared down the plughole! It was gone!

'Oh – my thimble, my thimble!' yelled Amelia Jane. But it was gone for good. Nobody ever saw it again.

'Serves you right, Amelia,' said the bear, turning the poor skittle the right way up again. 'Well, who would have thought the pixie knew a spell like that? Did *you* know that heat made things just a bit bigger, clockwork clown?'

'I never did,' said the clown.

But the funny thing is that it's *true*! So if ever a thimble gets stuck on one of your skittles you'll know what to do

– stand him on his head in hot water and it will slip off!

And now Amelia Jane can't *bear* doing her mending, because she hasn't got a thimble and she pricks her finger all the time. Still, as the toys tell her – it's her own fault!

Amelia Jane Gets Into Trouble

Amelia Jane, as you all know, is a very clever and very naughty doll. The toys could never keep pace with her tricks – but one day she got herself into trouble.

It happened like this. Billy came into the nursery and looked round for his soldier doll. 'Tom, where are you?' he said. 'I'm going to take you to tea with me this afternoon and I'm going

in *my* soldier things, too! We're going
to play with Betty and Dick, and
they're going to dress up as soldiers as
well. So, with you, we'll be four
soldiers! We'll have fun!'

He began looking for Tom, the
soldier. But before he could find him
his mother called out. 'Billy! Come
here a minute. I want you.'

Billy ran out. Amelia Jane sat up,
her eyes gleaming. 'Tom, don't you
go! They'll do
awful things to
you!'

'Oh
dear!' said
Tom, in
alarm.
Although
he was a

227

soldier doll, he wasn't at all brave really. 'Oh dear! I don't want to go. I really don't!'

'Well, I'll go instead,' said Amelia Jane, in a kind voice. 'I'll do you a good turn and put on your clothes and go instead of you. Would you like that?'

'Oh, yes!' said Tom. He stripped off his soldier clothes, and Amelia Jane dressed herself up in them. My word, she did look different. You should have seen her! She pranced about looking very smart in Tom's trousers and jacket. 'I'm grand! I'm brave!'

She began to rush at the toys, pretending to capture them. They didn't like it at all.

'Now stop that, Amelia Jane!' said the sailor doll. 'And take off those clothes. You know perfectly well that nobody will harm Tom if he goes out to tea – you've only said that because you want to dress up and prance about pretending to be a soldier. Take those clothes off.'

But all that Amelia Jane did was to rush at the toy clown and the sailor doll, and pretend to capture them. They were very cross indeed – but Amelia was bigger than they were, and it was difficult to stop her.

In rushed Billy. He caught hold of Amelia Jane, thinking she was Tom, his soldier doll. Out of the door he went at top speed, calling out, 'I'm ready, Mother! I'm just coming!'

Amelia Jane planned to have a wonderful time. She would go stalking Betty and Dick with Billy. She would take them prisoner. My goodness, Amelia Jane was going to have the time of her life!

But it didn't turn out quite like that. Billy, Betty and Dick got the gardener to hide Amelia Jane somewhere, so that they could stalk her and pounce on her and take her prisoner!

So Amelia was put into the middle of a bush by the gardener, and left there. The children began to hunt for her, going along in single file, leaping high in the air, and filling the garden with loud cries.

Amelia Jane shivered in the bush. How she hoped they wouldn't find her. She didn't mind stalking the others and pouncing on them – but she didn't want to be pounced on and taken prisoner herself!

Well, the children soon found her. They surrounded the bush, and Betty yelled out loudly: 'The enemy is hiding here! I see him! Come on, soldiers, come on!'

And they all pounced! Amelia Jane was pulled roughly from the bush and thrown to the ground.

'You're our prisoner!' yelled the
three, and ran round her. They didn't
even touch Amelia, but she thought
they were going to every time they
came.

'Let's tie him to a tree,' said Billy.
So they took Amelia and tied her to a
little tree.

'Funny sort of doll, this,' said Dick, looking closely at her. 'He's got a face more like a girl-doll than a boy-doll.'

'Now he's tied up. He can't get away. He's our prisoner,' said Betty.

But fortunately for Amelia Jane, the tea-bell rang loudly, and the three soldiers raced up to the house in glee.

Amelia Jane began to sob. She struggled with the knots that tied her, but they were tight and she couldn't undo even one of them. She was very frightened. How she wished she hadn't been silly enough to make Tom give her his clothes!

'I'm always doing silly things!' wept Amelia. 'I wish I didn't. Oh, what shall I do?'

She waited for the children to

come back. She waited and she waited. But they didn't come. Betty's mother had said she thought it was going to rain, so they could either play a *quiet* game of soldiers indoors, or a noisy game of snap, whichever they liked.

They chose snap, and forgot all about Amelia Jane, tied to the tree in the garden. In fact Billy forgot about her completely, and even went home without her! So there she was when darkness came, still tied up tightly, jumping in fright every time an owl came by and hooted.

The toys were surprised when Billy came home without Amelia Jane. He didn't say anything about leaving her behind until just before he went to bed. He was sitting in his pyjamas eating his supper in the nursery with his sister, when he suddenly gave a cry.

'What's the matter?' said his mother.

'It's Tom. I've forgotten to bring him home,' said Billy. 'We tied him up to a tree and then we went in to tea and I forgot all about him. He's still there, poor thing. And it's dark and rainy. Mother, I must go and get him.'

'No, you mustn't,' said his mother, firmly. 'You are certainly not going to run down the dark rainy street in your pyjamas. You can get Tom tomorrow. If he's under a tree he won't get very wet.'

'But he'll be frightened,' said Billy. 'He won't like it.'

'Well, that's your fault,' said his mother. 'When we forget things we often make others suffer as well as ourselves. You should have remembered to bring Tom home.'

Now, of course, the toys couldn't help hearing all this, because they were sitting round the nursery watching the children eat their supper. They were full of horror.

What! Amelia Jane tied up to a tree, left alone in the darkness and the rain! Naughty as she was, and cross as they felt with her, they were very sorry. When the children had gone to bed they got together in a corner and talked about it.

'I'll go and rescue her,' said Tom, bravely. 'I know the way. I've been to that house before.'

'But you haven't got any clothes on,' said the sailor doll. 'You'll get soaked. And it's frightening to go out in the dark at night. You might meet a fierce dog or a yowling cat who would pounce on you. Anyway, you're not very brave.'

'Oh, I know that,' said Tom, sadly. 'It's a pity to have to be a soldier doll and not feel brave. That's really why I'm going. I'm not brave, in fact I'm very frightened, but I feel I *ought* to be brave, so I'm going to rescue Amelia.'

'Well, that's very nice of you, after she tricked you into taking off your clothes and letting her go out to tea instead of you,' said the toy clown, patting Tom on the back. 'All right, you go then, if you know the way. What about clothes? There's a little

cape and hat in the doll's wardrobe.
You could borrow those.'

So Tom put them on and he looked
rather odd, not at all like a soldier
doll! Then he slipped out of the
window, climbed down the tree
outside and set off in the darkness to
Betty's house.

The rain hit him on the nose, and
ran down his cloak in little rivers. It
went down his neck too, because his
hat didn't fit very well. At last he
came to the garden of Betty's house
and slipped through a hole in the
fence.

Amelia Jane was still tied to the
tree. An owl had hooted in her ear. A
spider had walked over her face. A
hedgehog had walked so near that his
spines pricked her legs. She was lonely

and scared.

She heard a noise. What was that? Oh, what was that? It sounded like someone coming nearer and nearer, creeping through the bushes! Amelia began to tremble and shake.

'Who is it? Go away! Leave me alone! Oh, don't come near me, I'm scared, I'm frightened! Don't frighten me any more. Go away, whoever it is!'

But the footsteps came nearer and nearer, and then a head poked round a bush. Amelia Jane gave a scream.

'Go away! I'm frightened of you!'

Well it was Tom, of course, come to rescue her! 'It's all right,' he said. 'It's only me, Tom. I'll undo your knots, Amelia Jane.'

Amelia could have hugged him!

Dear, dear Tom! Oh, how could she have tricked him like that! She would always, always love him now.

He undid the knots. She stretched herself stiffly and then sneezed. 'Let's hurry home,' said Tom. 'You've caught a cold. I'll lead the way.'

Well, it wasn't long before they were both back in the nursery again, leaving little wet marks all over the floor. As soon as they got there Amelia Jane flung herself on Tom and hugged him so hard that he squealed.

'Good, kind, *brave* Tom! Oh, what courage you've got! Oh, how plucky you are! Toys, Tom is quite the bravest toy in the nursery!'

Tom could hardly believe his ears when all the toys crowded round and thumped him on the back, and said the same as Amelia! 'But I'm not brave!' he kept saying. 'I never have been! I was frightened all the time. Brave people aren't frightened.'

'The bravest people of all are those who are frightened and yet go on being brave,' said the sailor doll, helping him off with his wet cloak. 'Amelia Jane has no right to wear a soldier's clothes – she's a little coward! As soon as they are dry, you must wear them again, because you really and truly are a brave soldier!'

The toys dried Tom's clothes, as soon as Amelia Jane had taken them off. Amelia dressed humbly in her own clothes. She felt ashamed of herself. She sneezed loudly.

'I'm getting a dreadful cold,' she said, very sorry for herself.

'It serves you right,' said the sailor doll. 'Don't sneeze all over us, please. We're giving a party for Tom soon, and you'd better not come in case you give everyone your cold.'

So now Amelia Jane is sitting by herself in a corner sneezing into her hanky, watching the most wonderful party going on, given for Tom, the soldier doll. Nobody feels at all sorry for her. I don't know if you do?

Billy's going to be very surprised tomorrow to find that Tom is sitting in the nursery instead of tied up to the tree! He's going to puzzle about that for days.

Amelia Jane Has a Good Idea

The new teddy bear was very small
indeed. The toys stared at him when
he first came into the playroom,
wondering what he was.

'Good gracious! I believe you're a
teddy bear!' said Amelia Jane, the big,
naughty doll. 'I thought you were a
peculiar-shaped mouse.'

'Well, I'm not,' said the small bear,
sharply, and pressed himself in the

middle. 'Grrrrrr! Hear me growl? Well, no mouse can growl. It can only squeak.'

'Yes. You're a bear all right,' said Tom, coming up. 'I hear you've come to live with us. Well, I'll show you your place in the toy-cupboard – right at the back there, look.'

'I don't like being at the back, it's too dark,' said the little bear. 'I'll be at the front here, by this big brick-box.'

'Oh, no you won't. That's *my* place when I want to sit in the toy-cupboard,' said Amelia Jane. 'And let me tell you this, small bear – if you live with us you'll have to take on lots of little bits of work. We all do. You'll have to wind up the clockwork clown when he runs down, you'll have to clean the dolls'-house windows, and you'll have to help the engine-driver polish his big red train.'

'Dear me, I don't think I want to do any of those things,' said the bear. 'I'm lazy. I don't like working.'

'Well, you'll just have to,' said Amelia Jane. 'Otherwise you won't get any of the biscuit crumbs that the children drop on the floor, you won't get any of the sweets in the toy sweet-shop – and we're allowed some every week – and you won't come to any parties. So there.'

'Pooh!' said the bear and stalked off to pick up some beads out of the bead-box and thread himself a necklace.

'He's vain as well as lazy,' said Tom in disgust. 'Hey, bear – what's your name? Or are you too lazy to have one?'

'My name is Sidney Gordon Eustace,' said the bear, haughtily. 'And please remember that I don't like being called Sid.'

'Sid!' yelled all the toys at once, and the bear looked furious. He turned his head away, and went on threading the beads.

'Sidney Gordon Eustace!' said the clown, with a laugh. 'I guess he gave himself those names. No sensible child would ever call a teddy bear that. Huh!'

The bear was not much use in the playroom. He just would *not* do any of the jobs there at all. He went

surprisingly deaf when anyone called
to him to come and clean or polish or
sweep. He would pretend to be asleep,
or just walk about humming a little
tune as if nobody was calling his
name at all. It was most annoying.

'Sidney! Come and shake the mats
for the dolls'-house dolls!' Tom called.
No answer from Sidney at all.

'SIDNEY! Come here! You're not
as deaf as all that!'

The bear never even turned his
head.

'Hey, Sidney Gordon Eustace –
come and do your jobs!' yelled Tom.
'SID, SID, SID!'

No answer. 'All right!' shouted
Tom, angrily. 'You shan't have that
nice big crumb of chocolate biscuit we
found under the table this morning.'

It was always the same whenever there was a job to be done. 'Sidney, come here!' But Sidney never came. He never did one single thing for any of the toys.

'What are we going to do about him?' said the big teddy bear. 'Amelia Jane – can't you think of a good idea?'

'Oh, yes,' said Amelia at once. 'I know what we'll do. We'll get Sidney-the-mouse to come and do the things that Sidney-the-bear should do – and he shall have all the crumbs and titbits that the bear should have. He won't like that – a little house-mouse getting all his treats!'

'Dear me – is the house-mouse's name Sidney, too?' said Tom in surprise. 'I never knew that before.

When we want him we usually go to his hole and shout "Mouse" and he comes.'

'Well, I'll go and shout "Sidney",' said Amelia Jane, 'and you'll see – he'll come!' So she went to the little hole at the bottom of the wall near the bookcase and shouted down it.

'Sidney! Sid-Sid-Sidney! We want you!'

The little bear, of course, didn't turn round – *he* wasn't going to come when his name was called. But someone very small came scampering up the passage to the hole-entrance. It was the tiny brown house-mouse, with bright black eyes and twitching whiskers.

'Ah, Sidney,' said Amelia Jane. 'Will you just come and shake the mats in the dolls' house, please? They are very dusty. We'll give you a big chocolate biscuit crumb and a drink of lemonade out of the little teapot if you will.'

'Can I drink out of the spout?' said the tiny mouse, pleased. 'I like drinking out of the spout.'

'Yes, of course,' said Amelia Jane.

The little mouse set about shaking the mats vigorously, and the job was soon done.

'Isn't Sidney wonderful?' said Amelia in a loud voice to the others. 'Sidney-the-mouse, I mean, of course, not silly Sidney-the-bear. He wouldn't have the strength to shake mats like that, poor thing. Sidney, here's the chocolate biscuit crumb and there's the teapot full of lemonade.'

Sidney the bear didn't like this at all. Fancy making a fuss of a silly little mouse, and giving him treats like that. He would very much have liked the crumb and the lemonade himself. He pressed himself in the middle and growled furiously when the mouse had gone.

'Don't have that mouse here again,' he said. 'I don't like hearing somebody else being called Sidney. Anyway, I don't believe his name *is* Sidney. It's not a name for a mouse.'

'Well, for all you know, his name might be Sidney Gordon Eustace just like yours,' said Amelia Jane at once.

'Pooh! Whoever heard of a mouse having a grand name like that?' said the bear.

'Well, next time you won't do a job, we'll call all three names down the hole,' said Amelia, 'and see if the little mouse will answer to them!'

Next night there was going to be a party. Everyone had to help to get ready for it. Amelia Jane called to the little bear.

'Sidney! Come and set the tables for the party. Sidney, do you hear me?'

Sidney did, but he pretended not to, of course. Set party tables! Not he! So he went deaf again, and didn't even turn his head.

'Sidney Gordon Eustace, do as

you're told or you won't come to the party,' bawled the big teddy bear in a fine old rage.

The little bear didn't answer. Amelia Jane gave a sudden grin.

'Never mind,' she said. 'We'll get Sidney Gordon Eustace, the little mouse, to come and set the tables. He does them beautifully and never breaks a thing. He can come to the party afterwards then. I'll call him.'

The little bear turned his head. 'He won't answer to *that* name, you know he won't!' he said, scornfully. 'Call away! No mouse ever had a name as grand as mine.'

Amelia Jane went to the mouse-hole and called down it.

'Sidney Gordon Eustace, are you there?' she called. 'If you are at home,

come up and help us. Sidney Gordon
Eustace, are you there?'

And at once there came the
pattering of tiny feet, and with a loud
squeak the little mouse peeped out of
his hole, his whiskers quivering.

'Ah – you are at home,' said
Amelia. 'Well, dear little Sidney, will
you set the tables for us? We're going
to have a party.'

The mouse was delighted. He was
soon at work, and in a short while the
four tables were set with tiny table-
cloths and china. Then he went to
help the dolls'-house dolls to cut
sandwiches. The bear watched all this
out of the corner of his eye. He was
quite amazed that the mouse had
come when he was called Sidney
Gordon Eustace – goodness, fancy a

little mouse owning a name like that!

He was very cross when he saw
that the mouse was going to the
party. Amelia Jane found
him a red ribbon to tie
round his neck and
one for his
long tail. He
was given a place at the
biggest table, and
everyone made a fuss of him.

'Good little Sidney! You do work
well! Whatever should we do without
you? What will you have to eat?'

The mouse ate a lot. *Much* too
much, the little bear thought. He
didn't go to the party. He hadn't been
asked and he didn't quite like to go
because there was no chair for him
and no plate. But, oh, all those nice

things to eat! *Why* hadn't he been sensible and gone to set the tables?

'Goodnight, Sidney Gordon Eustace,' said Amelia to the delighted mouse. 'We've loved having you.'

Now, after this kind of thing had happened three or four times the bear got tired of it.

He hated hearing people yell for 'Sidney, Sidney!' down the mouse-hole, or to hear the mouse addressed as Sidney Gordon Eustace. It was really too bad. Also, the mouse was getting all the titbits and the treats. The bear didn't like that either.

So the next time that there was a job to be done the bear decided to do it. He suddenly heard Tom say 'Hallo! The big red engine is very smeary. It wants a polish again. I'll go and call Sidney.'

Tom went to the mouse-hole and began to call down it. 'Sidney, Sidney, Sidney!'

But before the mouse could answer, Sidney the bear rushed up to Tom. 'Yes! Did you call me? What do you want me to do?'

'Dear me – you're not as deaf as usual!' said Tom, surprised. 'Well, go and polish the red engine, then. You can have a sweet out of the toy sweet shop if you do it properly.'

Sidney did do it properly. Tom came and looked at the engine and so did Amelia Jane. 'Very nice,' said Amelia. 'Give him a big sweet, Tom.'

The bear was pleased. Aha! He had done the mouse out of a job. The toys had been pleased with him, and

the sweet was delicious.

And after that, dear me, you should have seen Sidney the bear rush up whenever his name was called. 'Yes, yes – here I am. What do you want me to do?'

Very soon the little mouse was not called up from the hole any more, and Sidney the bear worked hard and was friendly and sensible. The toys began to like him, and Sidney liked them too.

But one thing puzzled Tom and the big teddy bear, and they asked Amelia Jane about it.

'Amelia Jane – HOW did you know that the mouse's name was Sidney Gordon Eustace?'

'It isn't,' said Amelia with a grin.

'But it must be,' said Tom. 'He always came when you called him by it.'

'I know – but he'd come if you called *any* name down his hole,' said Amelia. 'Go and call what name you like – he'll come! It's the calling he answers, not the name! He doesn't even know what names are!'

'Good gracious!' said Tom and the bear, and they went to the mouse-hole.

'William!' called Tom, and up

came the mouse. He was given a
crumb and went down again.

'Polly-Wolly-Doodle!' shouted the
big bear, and up came the mouse for
another crumb.

'Boot-polish!' shouted Tom, and
up came the mouse.

'Tomato soup!' cried the big bear.

And it didn't matter what name was yelled down the hole, the mouse always came up. He came because he heard a loud shout, that was all. Amelia Jane went off into fits of laughter when the mouse came up at different calls. 'Penny stamp! Cough-drop! Sid-Sid-Sid! Dickory-Dock! Rub-a-dub-dub!'

The mouse's nose appeared at the hole each time. How the toys laughed – all except Sidney the bear!

He didn't laugh. He felt very silly indeed. Oh, dear – what a trick Amelia Jane had played on him! But suddenly he began to laugh, too. 'It's funny,' he cried. 'It's funny!'

It certainly was. Amelia *would* think of a good idea like that, wouldn't she?

Amelia Jane is Very Busy

One day Amelia Jane sat very still in her little chair, and watched somebody knitting in the playroom. It was little Miss Jones, who came to help with the children's clothes. She was knitting a jersey for the biggest boy.

'Click-click-clickety-click!' Her knitting needles flashed in and out all day long, and Amelia Jane watched and watched.

When little Miss Jones had finished all the knitting and had put the balls of left-over wool neatly in the work-basket with the long needles, she left the playroom to go home.

As soon as she had gone Amelia Jane ran to the work-basket. She took up two needles and a ball of wool and went to sit on the rug by herself, leaning against the table-leg.

'I can knit,' she told the toys. 'I know how to. I watched Miss Jones all day long. You go like this – and like that – and see,

the knitting comes!'

The toys watched her. They thought Amelia Jane was very clever. Click-click-clickity-click – why, her needles went as fast as Miss Jones' needles!

'What are you making?' asked the sailor doll.

'Nothing. I'm just knitting,' said Amelia.

'But you must be knitting *something*,' said the clockwork mouse. 'You can't just *knit*.'

'It's a waste of wool not to make something when you knit,' said the teddy bear. 'Can't you make me a jersey?'

'No. It would take me ages to knit a jersey to go over your fat little tummy,' said Amelia Jane.

'Don't be rude,' said the bear, offended. 'If *you* kept a growl in your tummy, you'd be fat, too. Grrr!'

'Couldn't you knit me a bonnet?' said the baby doll. 'I could do with a new one.'

'No, I couldn't. You've got three already,' said Amelia Jane. 'For goodness' sake go away and let me *knit*! I tell you, I'm not making anything at all, I'm just knitting.'

The baby doll sat down by her and took off her hair-ribbon to smooth it out. She was very particular about her ribbons. She put it down beside her, and began to comb out her hair with a little comb.

'Go away,' said Amelia. 'I don't like people who comb hair all over me.'

'Well, you can just put up with it,' said the baby doll, crossly. 'I can sit where I like.'

Amelia Jane didn't say anything – but when the baby doll looked for her hair-ribbon it had gone!

'You've taken it!' she said to Amelia. 'You mean thing. Give it back.'

'She can't. She's knitted it with the wool!' said Tom, pointing. And sure enough that bad Amelia Jane had taken the ribbon and knitted it – and there was the ribbon, right in the very middle of the knitting.

'I can't take it out,' said Amelia. 'It would spoil my beautiful knitting. You'll have to do without your ribbon now. It's your own fault.'

The baby doll went off, crying.

'Cry-baby!' said Amelia Jane, and went on knitting.

'Your knitting is nothing but a long, long scarf, very narrow,' said the bear. 'It's silly knitting. Nobody would wear a scarf like that.'

'Nobody's going to,' said Amelia Jane. 'I wish you would stop bothering me. Can't I knit if I want to?'

'The click-click noise makes me cross,' said the sailor doll.

'It doesn't take much to make you cross,' said Amelia. 'Clockwork mouse, what do *you* want? Don't you dare to nibble my wool!'

'I just want to watch you knit,' said the mouse, and he sat down close by. And will you believe it, that rascally Amelia Jane knitted his long tail into her knitting! The little mouse

suddenly found himself pulled
towards Amelia's knitting, and saw
his tail there!

Goodness, what a to-do there was!
The bear was very angry. 'You can't
do things like this, Amelia!' he said.

'I can,' she said. 'And I have. The
mouse can't have his tail back. It
belongs to my knitting now.'

But the sailor doll made her undo

the tail because the clockwork mouse was so upset.

'He can't hang on to your knitting by his tail,' he told Amelia Jane.

'You're very unkind and very silly. Just *look* at the enormous length of knitting you have done – all for nothing, too!'

The next thing he knew was that Amelia had pulled out his bootlaces and had knitted those, too! She would not give them back, either, and the sailor doll stamped round the nursery in a rage, his boots slipping off his feet every minute!

'She'll have to fall asleep sometime soon,' whispered the teddy bear to the toy soldier. 'Then we'll pay her out for all this!'

So they waited till her needles

worked more and more slowly –
clickity-click, clickity-click – click –
click – click – click – and then they
stopped. Amelia Jane was fast asleep!

The toys crept up to her. They
took up the long, long strip of
knitting. They wound it all round
Amelia Jane and the table-leg she was
leaning against – round and round
and round and round!

'Now she's all tied up in her own
knitting!' said Tom,
pleased. 'And the more
she knits, the more tied

up she will get.'

Amelia Jane woke up merry and bright. She picked up her knitting needles and started off again – clickity-click, clickity-click!

But soon she found that she was bound tightly to the table-leg, and the more she pulled at her knitting, the tighter it became. She tried to stand up – but she couldn't.

'Oh! Oh! I've knitted myself to the table-leg!' she cried. 'Toys, help me!'

'Certainly *not*,' said the clockwork clown with a squeal of delight. 'Go on knitting. You'll soon be right in the middle of it and we shan't see you again! Knit hard, Amelia, knit hard!'

Amelia Jane didn't. She stopped. She tugged at the knitting to try to free herself but she couldn't. And dear me, how scared she got when she saw how the knitting was wound round and round and round herself and the table-leg!

'Undo me!' she begged the baby doll.

'I will if you knit me a new bonnet,' said the doll.

'Undo me!' Amelia Jane begged the bear.

'I will if you knit me a jersey and don't say anything about my fat little tummy,' said the bear.

'And you can knit me a red waistcoat,' said Tom.

'And me a new vest,' said the sailor doll.

'All right,' said Amelia. 'You're mean, all of you. But I'll knit what you want – and I hope nothing fits, so there!'

Well, they undid Amelia Jane from the table-leg, and then they helped her to pull undone all the long, long piece of knitting.

Out came the sailor's bootlaces and the baby doll's ribbon!

And then she had to set to work to keep her promises. She has made the bear a tight little red jersey.

'You'll never be able to get it off

again, once you've got it on,' Tom told him, so the poor bear can't make up his mind whether to wear it or not.

Amelia has made the sailor a

new vest, but as it reaches down to his feet he doesn't quite know what to do with it!

As for Tom's waistcoat, it's got three armholes instead of two! 'Use one for a leg!' said Amelia with a giggle. But how can he do that?

And now Amelia is knitting the bonnet for the baby doll, but as it is already big enough to go all round the teddy bear's middle, I expect she will have to use it for a shawl!

Can't you be sensible, Amelia Jane – just for once? Tie her up to the table-leg again, toys! She's just too bad for words.

Oh, Bother
Amelia Jane!

'What are you doing, Amelia Jane?'
asked the sailor doll. 'What do you
want that water for?'

'I'm going to paint,' said Amelia.
'See, I've found a paint-box in the
toy-cupboard. I know how to paint
because I've watched the children.'

'How do you paint?' asked the
sailor doll.

Amelia Jane dipped her paint-

brush into the water and then rubbed
it on one of the little squares of colour
in the paint-box.

'I paint like this!' she said with a
giggle and splashed a big stripe of
green all across the sailor doll's face!

He was very angry. He went off to
tell the other toys. 'She's in one of her
silly moods again,' he said to Tom.
'We'd better look out!'

Amelia Jane painted hard all the morning. At first she painted pictures on a piece of paper. Then she looked round for something better to do with her paints.

'The dolls' house! I'll paint monkeys climbing up the wall,' she said. 'The little dolls have gone out for a walk – they'll be surprised when they come back!'

So she painted little brown monkeys all the way up the front walls of the pretty little dolls' house – they did look peculiar!

The dolls'-house dolls screamed when they came back. 'Look! What's that on the walls? Monkeys! Are they real? Oh, what's happened to our dear little house?'

'You be careful in case there are

monkeys inside it too!' said Amelia
Jane, and not one of the tiny dolls
dared to go in at their front door!

Then she saw the little wooden
train standing by itself in a corner of
the room. The engine-driver had gone
to talk to the teddy bear, so he wasn't
there. Amelia Jane took her pot of
water and paint-box – and do you
know what she did? She painted rows
of silly faces all round the engine and
its trucks!

'Look! What's happened? Where
did these dreadful faces come from?'
cried the engine-driver when he saw
them. 'My beautiful train! Everyone
will laugh at me when I drive it.'

'You'd better get a cloth and
rub all the faces off,' said Tom.
'Bother Amelia Jane! I'll help you,

Engine-driver.'

So they spent a long, long time trying to get the faces off the engine and the train. They were very hot and tired by the end of it.

'I'd be much obliged if you would go and give Amelia Jane a good telling-off from me,' said the engine-driver. 'I'm too small to do it myself.'

'With pleasure,' said Tom and he went up to Amelia Jane, and gave her a good scolding. She was very angry – and you can guess what she did! She painted his hat white when he was asleep!

It did look strange.

He was very much upset. All the toys stood round him and giggled.

'What happened?' said the teddy bear. 'Your hat's all white, Tom!'

Tom had to climb up to the little wash-basin, turn on a tap, put the plug in, and try to wash the white off his hat. He managed to get himself wet all over, and the white ran down his jacket and trousers.

So then he had to sit in front of the fire, and when his jacket dried it shrank and was so tight that he could hardly breathe. He was very, very cross with Amelia Jane!

She painted the clockwork mouse's tail a bright red, and he thought it was a worm running after him. He raced away, squealing, 'I can't get away from that red worm; it follows me, it follows me!' The toys couldn't help laughing.

'It's only your tail. Don't be afraid of your own tail,' said the bear. 'Go and climb up to the bookshelf, where the bowl of goldfish is. Sit on the edge and dip your tail into the water. The red will run off and you will be all right again.'

'Yes, you do that,' said Amelia Jane, with a grin. *She* knew what would happen, but the others didn't! The clockwork mouse got up on to the bookcase, and went to the goldfish bowl. He sat on the edge and dipped his red tail into the water.

The goldfish were very excited. 'A worm! A lovely long red worm!' they bubbled to one another. 'Quick, catch it and eat it!'

And they swam to the little red tail and snapped at it. Goodness – the mouse almost fell backwards into the water! 'Don't! Don't! That's

my tail!' he squealed.

He only just managed to get it out
of the bowl before it was nibbled off.
He raced down to the floor, tumbling
over and over when he got there.

Amelia Jane laughed and laughed.
The clockwork mouse cried bitterly. 'I
wish *you* had a tail!' he said to Amelia
Jane. 'I'd come and nibble it, then
you'd know how it felt!'

Now the next night, a small mouse, a real one this time, came running out of a hole in the playroom wall with a little note in his mouth. It was from the toys in the next house.

'I say!' said the clockwork clown, reading the note. 'The toys next door are giving a fancy dress party! What fun! It's the night after next. Well, *I* shall go as a pirate!'

'I shall go as one of the bears in the story of The Three Bears,' said the teddy bear.

'And I shall make myself a red cloak and hood and go as Red Riding Hood,' said the tiny doll in the corner of the toy-cupboard.

'I shall go as a queen,' said Amelia Jane, grandly. 'I can easily make myself a crown, and there's a beautiful dress laid away in a box in one of the drawers over there. I can make a cloak, and I have got a very pretty necklace that came out of a cracker.'

Well, Amelia Jane worked very hard indeed at making the lovely cloak. It was royal purple and she sewed tiny silver beads all over it, from the bead box. She tried on her crown – how lovely she looked! She put on the necklace.

'Don't I look beautiful?' she said to the other toys. 'I shall win the first prize for the fancy dress. I know I shall!'

Tom thought she probably would. 'You don't deserve to,' he said. 'You've been unkind. The clockwork mouse is still upset because the red hasn't properly come off his tail.'

'Pooh!' said Amelia Jane. 'You wait till I get the paint-box out again. I'll do MUCH worse things than that!'

That made the toys very angry. The bear decided to take the paint-box and hide it when Amelia wasn't looking. It was quite easy to do that because she was so tired that night with her hard work sewing on the silver beads that she fell asleep!

'Look at her – fast asleep!' said Tom. 'She doesn't *deserve* to win the first prize at the party. But she will!'

'She won't,' said the bear, suddenly. 'I've got an idea, Tom. Listen – *I* can paint just as well as Amelia Jane can. And I'm going to paint her face in all kinds of stripes and dots while she's asleep! It'll be red and blue and green and yellow!'

The toys stood and giggled as the bear took the paint-brush, dipped it into the little pot of water, and began to paint Amelia's sleeping face. Goodness, he did it well! Stripes of red and green, dots of blue and yellow, crosses of black and brown.

Oh dear – what a terrifying sight Amelia Jane looked!

'But she'll see herself in the mirror, won't she?' said the clockwork mouse.

'No, because she would have to climb up on the bookcase, and stand there to see herself in the mirror on the wall,' said the bear. 'And she won't do that when she's wearing a cloak. She couldn't climb in that.'

Well, when Amelia Jane woke up,

she didn't know anything about her painted face, of course. All the toys put on fancy dresses for the party – and Amelia Jane couldn't *think* why they giggled every time they looked at her. In fact the clockwork mouse laughed so much that his key fell out.

Amelia walked up and down, wearing her crown and necklace, with the beautiful silk dress going 'swish-swish-swish' all the time, and her cloak flying out behind her, gleaming with silver beads. She didn't know how funny she looked, with her painted face, all stripes and dots and crosses!

'First prize for *me*!' she said to the

toys. 'Don't you think so?'

That made them giggle again, of course. Amelia Jane simply couldn't understand them. 'You're being very silly tonight,' she said. 'Well – I'm just going out into the passage to look at myself in the long mirror there. I don't want to climb up to the bookcase mirror in this long cloak.'

The toys had quite forgotten *that* mirror! They wondered whatever Amelia Jane would say when she saw herself. She walked out into the passage – and then she gave a loud scream.

'Oh! OH! My face! What's happened to it? Oh, you wicked bad toys, you've painted it! And I haven't time to wash it off properly. Oh, you horrid mean things.'

'We've only done to you what you did to us!' said Tom, grinning. 'You can't go to the party like that – and it serves you right!'

'I shall come! I shall! You just see!' cried Amelia Jane, and she took off her crown and necklace and began to undo her cloak. 'Yes, and I'll get first prize, too! Oh, you unkind things!'

'Well, we won't wait. It's time we set off,' said the bear. 'Goodbye, Amelia Jane. We are sorry we shan't see you at the fancy dress party.'

But all the same Amelia is going! I look like an Indian, with war-paint on my face! she thought, as she threw off her lovely dress. All right – I'll go as an Indian! Where's that little shuttlecock with coloured feathers set round it? They will do for my hair!

She pulled out the feathers and set them round her head. Then she looked for the little wigwam tent that the bear and Tom sometimes played with. It was painted brightly.

'That will do for a cloak,' said Amelia. 'And where's that rubber axe? Ah, here it is – that shall be my tomahawk! And who shall be my enemies? The toy soldier, the bear and all the rest! Look out – I'm coming to the party after all!'

And off she went at top speed, the fiercest Indian you ever saw. What a shock the toys are going to get! I can only hope that naughty Amelia Jane doesn't win the first prize after all!

Goodbye, Amelia Jane!

The toys played a trick on Amelia Jane the other day.

Amelia Jane was always playing tricks on all the toys in the nursery. There was no end to her mischief. If she didn't think of one thing, she thought of another.

There was the time when she collected worms in the garden and popped them all into Tom's shut umbrella. They wriggled about there and couldn't get out, poor things.

And then Amelia sent Tom out into the garden to fetch her hanky from the garden seat. It was raining, of course, so she gave him his umbrella.

'Better put this up,' she said, and he did. And out slithered all the worms, on top of his head and down his neck, as soon as he got out into the garden in the rain.

The worms fled into holes very

thankfully, but Tom got such a fright that he ran straight into the pond and got wet through.

He was very, very angry with Amelia Jane, but she only laughed.

'You shouldn't let worms nest in your umbrella,' she said.

Another time, Amelia took the teapot out of the toy tea-set and filled it with hot water from the tap. Then she climbed up to the roof of the dolls' house and poured the hot

water down the chimney.

The little dolls'-house dolls rushed out of the front door in fright, with water trickling down the stairs after them, and Amelia Jane nearly fell off the roof with laughing.

She was well scolded for that bit of mischief, but she wouldn't even say she was sorry.

The toys had a meeting about her.

'I'm tired of Amelia Jane,' said the toy soldier.

'So am I,' said the clockwork clown. 'She took my key away yesterday for about the fiftieth time.'

'Can't we get rid of her?' said the teddy bear.

'We've often tried,' said the clockwork mouse. 'But we never have.'

'I've got an idea,' said Tom, his

eyes shining brightly. 'It's a small idea at the moment – but if we talk about it, it might grow into a big one and be really good.'

'What is it?' asked the clockwork clown.

'Well – you know you can slide down the stairs on a tray, don't you?' said Tom.

Everyone nodded.

'That's my idea,' said Tom. 'It's only just that. I haven't thought any more than that.'

'It seems rather silly,' said the bear. 'Did you mean to get Amelia Jane to slide down the stairs on a tray, or what?'

'I don't know,' said Tom. 'I tell you, I hadn't thought any further than I said.'

'Ooooh!' said the clown. '*Could* we make her slide down on a tray – push her very, very hard . . . ?'

'And have the front door open so that she shot right out in a hurry,' went on the bear.

'And have the garden gate open so that she'd shoot out there, too,' said the clown.

'And then down the hill she'd go, whizz-bang, faster and faster and faster,' said the clockwork mouse, excitedly.

'And splash into the stream on her tray, and off it would go like a boat, all the way down to the sea!' finished Tom, his face beaming with excitement.

'And we'd never, never see her again, the bad, naughty doll,' said the bear.

'No, we wouldn't. We'd shout,

"Goodbye, Amelia Jane!" when she flew out of the front door, and that would be that,' said Tom. 'See what my little idea has grown to – a great big one. I thought it would!'

Well, the toys talked and talked about their idea, and got very excited about it indeed. Surely they could at last get rid of that naughty Amelia Jane!

Amelia didn't know anything about all this, of course. She was out in the garden collecting a few more worms to play another trick. Tom had time to get out the big tin tray from its corner and rub soap underneath it to make it more slippery.

'We'll play our trick when everyone is out tomorrow,' he decided. 'If I stand on a chair in the hall I can open the front door all right. Now, don't say a word about our plan, any of you!'

The next afternoon the house was very quiet because everyone had gone out. Tom took the tin tray and banged hard on it. 'Boom, diddy-boom!'

'Stop that noise,' said Amelia Jane, crossly. 'I want to have a snooze.'

'All right. Have one,' said Tom. 'We are all going to the top of the stairs to play at sliding down on this tea-tray. We'll have a lovely time – and we don't want *you*, Amelia Jane!'

Well, that was quite enough to make Amelia want to come, of course! 'I'm coming, too,' she said. 'And I guess I'll go faster down the stairs than any of you!'

Off they all went to the top of the stairs. Tom ran down, got a chair, stood on it, and opened the front door. He ran back and had his turn at sliding down. The tray went down to the bottom, bumpity-bumpity-bump, slid a little way down the hall and stopped. Aha! If they all pushed hard when Amelia Jane had her turn, it would most certainly fly out of the door, down the path, out of the gate and away down the hill to the stream at the bottom!

'I want my turn, I want mine!' shouted Amelia, and she got on to the tray. She held tight – and the toy soldier, the bear, the clockwork clown, the mouse and another doll all pushed as hard as ever they could.

Whoooooosh! You should have

seen that tray fly down the stairs at top speed! Amelia's breath was quite taken away. Her hair and her dress flew out behind her, and she stared in fright. This was a much faster journey than she had imagined!

Down to the bottom of the stairs – along the hall at top speed – out of the open door – down the slippery front path – out of the open gate – and whooooooosh – down the steep hill that led to the stream!

'Goodbye, Amelia Jane!' shouted the toys. 'Goodbye, goodbye!'

'She's gone,' said the bear, after a pause. 'Really gone. She'll never tease us again.'

'Never,' said Tom, pleased. 'She's played her last trick on us.'

'She deserved to be shot off like

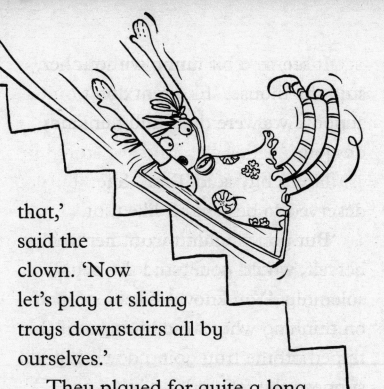

'that,'
said the
clown. 'Now
let's play at sliding
trays downstairs all by
ourselves.'

They played for quite a long
time. Then they went back to the
nursery to have a drink of water.

'I just hope Amelia Jane didn't tip
off the tray going down the hill, and
hurt herself,' said the bear, suddenly.

'And I just hope she didn't fall into
the stream and get drowned,' said the
clown.

'It seems a bit funny without her,' said the mouse. 'Er – you don't suppose we were dreadfully unkind, do you?'

'Not a bit,' said Tom. 'She deserved to be sent off like that.'

'But you wouldn't want her to hurt herself, would you?' said the bear, solemnly. 'You know – I keep on and on thinking what would happen if she tipped off the tray going down-hill – suppose she fell under a bus – or . . .'

The clockwork mouse gave a squeal of fright. 'Don't say things like that. They frighten me. You make me feel as if I want Amelia Jane back.'

'Perhaps she wasn't as bad as she seemed,' said the bear. 'You know – I don't feel very nice about playing that trick on her now. I feel sort of uncomfortable.'

'Pooh!' said Tom, but he didn't say any more.

Well, what *had* happened to Amelia Jane? She had slid out into the front garden and out of the gate, and down the hill at top speed. She was very frightened indeed. Why had the toys shouted goodbye? Was it a trick they had played on her to get rid of her? Amelia Jane wailed aloud as she shot down the hill. Oh dear, oh dear, had she been so dreadful that the toys wanted to get rid of her like that?

'I'm going straight into the stream!' she squealed, and splash, into the water she went. She clung to the tray. It didn't sink, but bobbed on the surface, with a very wet Amelia

Jane clinging on top. Down the stream she went, bobbing on the waves.

She floated for a very long way. Then the tray bumped into the bank, stuck into some weeds and stopped. Amelia thankfully crawled off on to the land. She was wet and cold and tired. She could see a dog not far off and she was frightened of him.

Where could she hide? What was that lying on the grass over there? A bicycle! It had a basket behind the saddle, and Amelia Jane staggered off to it. She squeezed into the basket, and stuffed an old bit of newspaper over herself. Now, perhaps, nobody, not even the dog, would see her.

She fell asleep and dreamed of the toys. She dreamt that they were all cross with her, and she cried in her sleep.

'Don't be cross with me. I'll be good, I'll be good.'

Then she woke up – and dear me, she was wobbling from side to side in the basket. Somebody had picked up the bicycle, mounted it, and was now riding away down the river path – with Amelia Jane tucked into the basket at the back.

Oh, dear! thought Amelia, in a panic. 'Now where am I going? I'm miles and miles away from home – and from all the toys. I wish I was back again. Wouldn't I be good if I could only get back to the nursery! But the toys wouldn't be pleased to see me at all. They'd turn me out again.'

On she went and on. Miles and miles it seemed to Amelia Jane, and she grew cramped and cold in the basket. And then, at last, the rider stopped and jumped off.

He flung his bicycle against something, and walked off, whistling.

Amelia Jane peeped out. The bicycle was against a wall near a back door. She crawled out of the basket, and almost fell to the ground. She ran to the door. If only she could get into a house, she could hide.

In she went, and somebody jumped in surprise as the big doll ran past. Amelia tore into the hall and up the stairs. She almost fell inside a room, and stopped there, panting in fright.

And will you believe it, she was

back in the nursery again – and there were all the toys she knew, staring at her in amazement – the toy soldier, the bear, the clown, the mouse and everyone!

She had come all the way home in the basket of the bicycle belonging to one of the children! He had gone to the river that day, and then had cycled all the way back – and Amelia Jane was in his basket. What a very, very peculiar thing!

'You said goodbye to me – but here I am again,' said Amelia, in a funny, shaky sort of voice. 'It seems as if you c-c-c-can't get rid of me!'

She burst into tears – and then everyone ran to comfort her. She was patted and fussed, and even Tom kept saying he was glad to see her back.

'Oh, dear – this is all so nice,' said Amelia at last. 'I won't be mischievous again, toys. I won't play tricks any more. I'll be just as good as gold!'

'We don't believe you,' said Tom. 'But never mind – we're glad to have you back, you bad, naughty doll. We never *really* want to say goodbye to you, Amelia Jane!'

I don't either. What about you?

EGMONT PRESS: ETHICAL PUBLISHING

Egmont Press is about turning writers into successful authors and children into passionate readers – producing books that enrich and entertain. As a responsible children's publisher, we go even further, considering the world in which our consumers are growing up.

Safety First
Naturally, all of our books meet legal safety requirements. But we go further than this; every book with play value is tested to the highest standards – if it fails, it's back to the drawing-board.

Made Fairly
We are working to ensure that the workers involved in our supply chain – the people that make our books – are treated with fairness and respect.

Responsible Forestry
We are committed to ensuring all our papers come from environmentally and socially responsible forest sources.

For more information, please visit our website at
www.egmont.co.uk/ethicalpublishing